*Take Me
To The
Underground*

Take Me To The Underground

by Renee Hansen

THE CROSSING PRESS
Freedom, California 95019

*Special thanks to Rena Zaid, Adrienne Alexander,
Julie Hall, Ann Tashi Slater, my brother John, and
Irene Zahava at The Crossing Press.*

Cover photograph by Susan Reich
Cover design by Betsy Bayley
Typesetting by Word Wise

Printed in the U.S.A.

Library of Congress Cataloging-in-Publication Data

Hansen, Renee.
    Take me to the underground / Renee Hansen.
      p.   cm.
      ISBN 0-89594-425-1 — ISBN 0-89594-399-9 (pbk.)
      I. Title.
    PS3558.A51325T3   1990   89-77276
    813' .54—dc20   CIP

You didn't have to attract desire. Either it was in the woman who aroused it or it didn't exist. Either it was there at first glance or else it had never been. It was instant knowledge of sexual relationship or it was nothing. That too I knew before I experienced it.

—Marguerite Duras
The Lover

I am attracted to her at all times. I am attracted to her and her dramatic arrivals in her dark baggy pants, blue dinner jackets and white starched collars. I am attracted to her when she appears weaker, when her legs and her arms are exposed in the loose khaki army shorts and the black tank top, when she is curled in my lap waiting for my touch—such as the time in the Cadillac.

In the Cadillac we have everything to talk about; we have nothing. Everything between us by now is understood. Our approaches are understood. Our partings—understood. It is the sixth or seventh or eighth time we have come together (made a "date") to break up. It is all either frighteningly intelligent, or frighteningly insane.

And so it is Saturday night and I come by, as arranged, to have our last "talk." I honk the horn. She comes out, with face pearlized by the street lamp. She is beautiful. Yes, I have ALWAYS thought that. I am nervous. How long have we gone out? One year? And I am still nervous. I'm still worried about what she thinks of me—even in the break-up. She practically skips out of the courtyard. She shouldn't be skipping. She shouldn't look so god damned thick and healthy on a summer night. She opens the door, peeks in, says, "You look good!" True, I've worn the black harem pants, the black cropped Tee. She slips into the passenger seat and stares at her hands. I am parked under boughs of linden trees, full moon tonight too, and the street lamp on the corner makes it all too beautiful and sad. Fuck. It should have been romance. Instead we are breaking up. And that really kills me. It really does. That I call her and say "We must break up," and she says, "You're right. It can't go any further. Come by." Just like that, she agrees, so easily. I conclude it was my energy keeping us together—always was.

And I do make a date to come by and break up. I always do. I come by when she says come by and I leave when she says leave. I do all that crazy stuff. From the car I can see the dog's head framed in the apartment window. I used to play with that dog and I really got to like him. Anyway, he's their dog now, Dorey will live with Ann now. Ann is up there now. Ann the beautiful Syrian woman with dark green eyes and a gravity I don't have. I don't know why she wants Ann, but she does. That happens sometimes. You fall in love with someone and it turns out they want someone else. But this story has a hitch in it, it certainly does. Dorey loves ME. That's what she says. She says she loves me but that I am too much for her and that Ann is quieter and Ann needs her more and Ann will love her forever and ever and so she is supposed to be with Ann for now and I am supposed to understand that. I don't. Ann does. Ann has agreed—quietly and with that ethereal dignity of hers—that Dorey should continue to go out with me and her—both. She wishes us much happiness together—all of us.

What kind of shit is that? That's what I asked Dorey when I first heard about that scheme and called her in a panic. "What does that mean, exactly?" I asked. "Does it mean that she will fade from the picture when you and I become more serious? Does it mean that she will never fade from the picture? That the three of us are supposed to fall in love? What kind of shit is that? Exactly what kind of shit? It's a mess," I said. "And the civility, the conviviality of it kills me at times. It's a fucking mess." I hung up on her, then called her back.

"I suppose we'll have two bedrooms?" I said on the phone. For one second I was considering it, and I wanted to know how the mechanics of the situation were being set up. "Yes," she responded.

"And the second one is for me?" I asked.

She was silent—irritated. "The second one is for whomever I choose to have over."

"Jesus, Dorey," I said. "What happened to the days when you dated a girl and you sort of fell in love. And you kept dating and then you lived together and then you were married? Can't we at least try that?"

"I can't," said Dorey. "I need you both."

So that's the way it was. I don't know why I couldn't leave Dorey, but I couldn't. I couldn't leave her just like she couldn't leave Ann. I was sure that Dorey held some secret to life, to me. And that once I got to know Dorey I would know about life. Once I got Dorey, everything would make sense, and I wouldn't be afraid of anything anymore. I think she felt the same way about Ann.

"I can't," I said to her. "I don't know why I can't

be so enlightened as to have this menage à trois but I can't," I told her over the phone late one evening; it was our eighth or ninth late evening phone call—and immediately I regretted it. Still, at that point, with some solemnity, frustration and too much fucking sadness, I made arrangements with Dorey to break it off.

And so this is why I drive by in the Cadillac. I study her in the seat next to me. I am always studying her. She always accused me of that. It is true. To me, it is always a nearly paralytic experience to be next to her. Her skin is silvery, like the night. She sits with her legs comfortably spread, in those large baggy shorts, dark tank top. She is a mess, as always, a handsome, beautiful, womanly mess . . . And I wish that I have come to pick her up for a date or something. I wish that we were going to the $1.75 movie. But it isn't like that. She opens and slams the door, I suppose out of nervousness. Her shoulder is pressed against the window, her hair combed back neatly. I like it messed-up, but who am I to say. I mean maybe Ann had combed it for her on her way out the door to see me. Maybe Ann had said, "Take care, darling," and Dorey had said, "I'll be back soon, just as soon as I can," and Ann had certainly known that she was coming down to see me but Ann had kissed her on the way out and brushed her hair aside anyway. And so I kept looking at the strands curled behind her ears. She never wears it that way. Ann did that. Fuck. Anyway, Dorey slides closer to me and sort of collapses across the seat so that her head is in my lap. At some point later, when I am feeling very stupid, I wonder how she could have been so god damned sure I wouldn't kick her out of the car.

But I do not kick her out of the car. Instead, I reach down and send my hand up her scalp. All of her hair comes down in her eyes. Messed, like I like it. She reaches up with her hand to grab mine. "I'm sorry," she says. I think she is crying. I begin to calculate a way back IN. Right away I think: "She knows I love her and she loves me and so I can mess her hair if I want to. And if I touch her she will know. She will know we belong together." Which equates to: "I can get her back if I want to." But I can't. Not really.

I hate her for saying I'm sorry. It means I have to be nice to her.

We sit in silence. She sits up and turns to me finally. She says, "You've come to tell me something?"

I shake my head yes.

"You know it doesn't have to be this way."

"Oh god, Dorey. We've been over this a thousand times . . . " I start crying or something.

"Shhh, shhh, shhh, shhhh," she says. "Not now, please." She touches me. I don't know why that should be so powerful, but it is. She puts her hand on my cheek and I think that I am safe.

Her head is in my lap again. I keep taking her hair in my fingers. It's so thick, so black . . . "Break up with Ann," I want to say—and feel silly. Ann isn't even our problem. Something else is our problem.

In the silence I keep pulling up strands of her hair between my fingers. She does nothing, says nothing. She looks drugged and is like a drug to me when I look at her. She is like a heavy, luscious sleep sometimes.

"I will always think you were mine." I say this as I gaze into the street—and the trees blowing up and down the block with the silvery leaves of a full-moon night make me believe all that. So I say it again: "You will always be mine. ALWAYS."

"I believe that you should have been mine," I continue. "I will always believe that a god made it this way. WE were meant to be and somehow cannot— and during this time we have somehow fucked it up in every way possible. And yet we *love* each other. I can't make it fit."

Dorey sits up quickly and clutches her head in her hands. She seems miserable. "It's you I love!"

"Then why the hell aren't we together? I mean, I can't figure it out. I mean don't you think it's strange, even slightly unethical to love one and live with another?"

She begins to shake violently and rock back and forth. She looks at me with rage that makes her face go white. Then she calms and says, "I can't talk to you anymore. I love you. I do. I love Ann too. You know that I need her right now, so why are you giving me such a hard time? I promise you it will end with Ann. I know it will. You know it will. Can't you just be patient and try to understand why I'm doing it?"

"Fuck you. I don't understand."

"I've been explaining it for a year."

"Explain it again."

"She supports me. She believes in me. She'll be there for me. I can't explain it. She'll be there for me in ways that you will not."

"Explain it again."

"You'll leave me. I swear. You're only going

through this love thing with me—because you want to go through it. I know you. You're in love with love. Once you get to know me, you'll leave."

This line always shut me up, because in a way, I had an inkling that Dorey was right about this.

Sometimes I didn't know why I had to have her. She was too beautiful. That was a good reason. And I thought she understood me. She understood my soul.

"Alexandra, I love you. You're making it difficult. Ann has agreed with me. She too thinks you are important to me. That you should be with me."

"I do understand," I shout back. "For Christ's sake, I've analyzed it for nearly a year. I'm probably the only person in the world who would understand this shit! Jesus, I can't believe you've discussed all this with Ann . . . and I'll say it again . . . I can't see you if you're living with her. I can't. I don't know why not. It's fucked. It's just too fucked."

"But she knows we are in love."

"I don't think you, nor her, nor I, know what love is anymore. We have fucked this up, royally. I don't even know how to relate to you . . . all I know how to do is relate to this relationship. All I know how to do is make relationship deals. And this is the latest and the saddest. I'm supposed to allow you to live with her for a few years until you're ready for me? Is that the deal?"

"It's YOU I want."

"Then live with me! God damn it!"

"I can't."

"Why not?"

"You know too much."

"What the fuck does that mean?"

"It means you know too much. About me."

"And so I can't live with you?"

"That's right. Ann is different. Things are simpler with Ann. With you I'm always talking about ethics! And morals! And how our damned souls understand each other. With her I talk about what I did that day. It is so simple."

"It's oppressive. You want to marry two women!"

"What's wrong with that!"

"I don't know. Something. Just . . . something . . . "

There is silence between us.

"It's gotten to be so perverse," I say. I am nearly crying.

She sits up. Her body is pressed into mine. "I don't want it to be so perverse," she whispers into my ear. "I only want you to be perverse." She says this as her fingers lay hold of the back of my neck, squeezing down.

I begin crying. "I NEED you god damn it! I need you! I need you. I need you. I need you."

"Shhhhhh. You don't," she whispers.

"Fuck you," I cry. "I need you."

"Don't cry. Don't cry." She is kissing my tears away. "Don't cry, baby."

"Please, you know. You know it, don't you? That I love you with my life. No one else will ever understand me the way you do."

"Alexandra, sometimes I think you've only read all this in your books." She is whispering, still licking, still kissing and sucking at my tears.

"God, I NEED you. Forget about the god damned books."

"Alexandra, stop. Please, stop." She is playing

8

with my hair. She is putting it behind my ears. And I think indignantly that she shouldn't do that if she isn't going to stay with me.

"You can go now," I say. "I'll be OK. Just go." And just like that she is out the door.

There were moments. There were moments with her that I like to remember, to dwell upon, to obsess upon. I believed life was contained in these moments. And they filled me. They filled like the hot vague orgasms of my dreams. I called them "Perfect Moments." And they were intoxicating. Heady. Very heady. They were so clear, these moments. They had lives of their own. I remember . . . I spend a lot of time remembering. Remembering brings it all back again.

I remember . . . In the morning I would watch Dorey awaken. White sheets between her legs and summer sun slanting across the sheet. Beautiful. "My baby," I would think. There she was asleep . . . breathing. A miracle.

Later, after breakfast, after making love, after a slow day, the slowest of days, Dorey would go to the bathroom sink, and throw her head under the faucet, and come out, water dripping down her back. She liked to make love this way, in the hall, on the floor, dripping all over me.

We would go out late, sometimes to the women's

bars, for drinks. And sometimes a woman would come up to us offering to buy us drinks. "Do women buy couples drinks?" I asked innocently the first time it happened.

"It's our sex," Dorey explained. "Everyone wants it."

I looked at her like she was crazy.

"They feel it," she said.

We would accept the drinks. It perpetuated our own myth to do so.

And then there was the artist's loft party. There was champagne, there were artists in black, there was the evening sun as we stood by the window, feeding each other small crackers with paté. Dorey had a turban on that night—dark eye make-up. We were watched. We were the lesbian couple who "looked so good together." We had been told that twice that evening.

There was a bowl of white husked grapes on the clavinova. There was Nancy, the clavinova player, on the stool, with long hands, full lips, and white-blond hair jutting out into the air. She cracked her knuckles and dedicated her song to the two beautiful women over there by the window. I guess Dorey and I stopped eating and laughed. She winked at us. But we all believed it. Dorey and I believed we were the two beautiful women and that just by being together we were creating the fantasies people lived by and fucked by.

Later, it will occur to me that we were primarily sexual communicators and that this was primarily because we were paralyzed in every other area of our lives. And later I will think, "Was that so bad?"

I remember . . . She took me standing in front of the mirror by the door of my apartment. I had a dress on. We were ready to go. "Don't move," she said. "Shhhhh." She took her hand and went up my dress. She kept telling me not to move. She grabbed my head and held it so that I could only stare in the mirror. She did it that way—kept telling me not to move, until finally, I collapsed.

Once, afterwards, we were lying in bed and Dorey began to run her finger in a circle around my breast, telling me a story. "I saw a large black horse eating in the field . . . and when I approached it I saw you lying near, unconscious, in the grasses. The horse had thrown you. I dragged you off to a cave in the mounds which was my secret place. I took off your boots and washed your feet. I took off all your clothes and looked at you. I drank some wine and stared at you all night. And finally, near morning, I began to make love to you. And I whispered in your ear that I would make you well and you would never see the outside world again.

"How does that sound?" she asked when she had finished.

"I want to hear more."

"Shhhhh. You can't talk now. You are unconscious and I am looking. Close your eyes," she said. And I did.

Dorey will say that I spend too much time dwelling on our past moments, glorifying them, bringing them up and up, and up. She will argue that she couldn't possibly be the woman of my "moments." She complains that our dates are never right. One of us is always overdressed. One of us will be in a foul mood, one of us will be tired and not feel like talking— or the restaurant will be all wrong. "This is reality," Dorey will say. "In reality we fuck everything up. It's only in your 'moments' that we love perfectly."

In a way she is right. Once we went to dinner at the Riverfront Club. The chairs were too large, they were arm chairs, and they bothered me because I felt small in them. I mean they were more like car seats than chairs and they swiveled and Dorey started swiveling in them as soon as she sat down—which also bothered me. And the table was large and I felt as if I were canyons away from her and I knew it wouldn't do. It wouldn't do at all. It was a Friday and we had reservations but as soon as we sat down I got up and announced that the chairs were awful and I couldn't sit in them all night. And that we had to go. "Why?" she asked.

"The chairs make me feel like a little person. It's all wrong," I said.

"Well, I don't want to go," she said, snapping out her napkin and smoothing it on her lap.

"We're going," I said and yanked at her hand.

And so we left. I think we ended up eating at McDonald's. It was a modern, silvery one and I didn't like it either.

I remember . . . We were on the beach once, in Florida. A warm day in the middle of January. We walked along the sand, she with a towel slung around her waist, a turban, a camera; me with white Bermuda shorts and bathing suit top. I carried a paper bag filled with bananas and Evian spring water, an old radio, keys to the car. We came upon a Wendy's, just built there in the sand. Brand new. It was like a fortress: square, brick and foreboding. Not a soul on its patio or standing at the salad bar inside. "Are we in another land?" I asked. She took my hand and led me past the Wendy's to strips of low-rise pink and yellow and blue condo buildings, one with a huge, aqua-blue dolphin arched over the top. I watched her feet make marks in the sand. "Where are we going?" I asked.

"There's a place around here. You'll see. I found it yesterday, driving. You'll see."

And then past more strips of blue and yellow and pink condos and some old people fishing on the beach, and then it was there, a park, an abandoned state park, or something. It was a strip of grassland with small hilly dunes and it went on for miles. And we found a dune, actually we found the crevice between two dunes and we lay the towel down in a neat square and put our shoes at the corners and put up a stick with a paper bag attached to it as our flag and put on the radio which was nearly all static, to a swing station, which was perfect—and made love— which was perfect—as I could hear the waves as I rocked and lost track of the waves within me and the waves outside of me.

I remember . . . She asked me once: "What if I can't be the one, Alexandra?"

"You ARE the one."

"But what if I failed you in the future?"

"You couldn't. Failure is impossible. All you have to do is BE with me. You are like a religion in me. I will never *not* believe that you were not the one."

But we did break up—in the Cadillac that evening . . . and I had every intention of it being a permanent break-up. So, for two years I am away from her. For two years I remember every glorious perfect moment. And then I get tired of it. I just get tired of living back there and not living in the now. And during this time I decide that I would like nothing better than to meet a regular girl with regular-type values and settle down and get married. And during this time I meet Lisa. Lisa likes to take walks. She likes to paint. She works at a camera shop. Everyone likes her there. Everyone likes Lisa, period. *I* like Lisa. We keep going out and keep going out. And two years after that scene in the Cadillac with Dorey, I find myself living with Lisa. I find myself loving Lisa and being in a different kind of love, saying "I love you," and everything. We buy a home together, we shop with our charge cards, and buy groceries out of a joint checking account. We subscribe to the *New York Times* and make spinach souffles on Sunday. On winter nights we play chess and eat chocolate chip cookies. We buy a 27-inch color TV with VCR, and rent nature films, and Disney films, and old Garbo and Dietrich films. After the films we go to bed. We make love. Our love is grand in a small way. It is entirely satisfying.

It happens when I am at my office one day after class. I am grading papers and the T.A. brings by the note. It says: "Can we meet? At the Art Institute? Two o'clock? Dorey."

I go. I am curious. "It can be friendship with Dorey," I tell myself. It is spring. She sits in the courtyard restaurant of the museum. And I can tell— I am saying to myself as I approach—"She is still handsome."

There is a yellow umbrella over the table. The table is near the fountain. In the fountain there is a statue of a young boy in knickers. He is playing with a goose, trying to grab hold of its belly with one hand, its neck with the other. From the panicked mouth of the goose springs a stream of water.

And Dorey? Dorey, on this hottest of spring days wears all black: black stretch pants, black sweater, black Reebok gym shoes. The thick skin of her hand presses into mine in greeting and there is this long pause as she holds my hand. She has dark sunglasses on. Too cool. Sometimes she is too cool.

"How are you?" she says.

"Fine, and you?" I nearly bow.

"Fine. Very good." The waiter brings a colander of Brandy Alexanders and two glasses. He pours as another waiter brings a basket of fruit, cheese paté and crackers.

"I ordered for us. I hope you don't mind," she says, just like that. Just so cool.

We drink the Brandy Alexanders and when we are finished we order a bottle of champagne. What the hell. Why not. We are already celebrating, you see. We get drunk in the afternoon underneath the umbrella. At four p.m. violinists arrive to play to the late afternoon crowd.

She leans over toward me. "I wouldn't think we could get together again. But I had to see you. I've thought about you. Many times I thought about you." And there is a by-the-way: "Ann is gone. We broke up months ago. And then I started thinking of you. I still love you. And this may sound terrible but I tried to stop loving you. I can't."

I try to take her last comment casually. But it is not casual . . . it is already serious. I am trying to think of ways to pass it up, to say, "You are too late." I can't.

We begin to see each other and I try to head off the impact. "Casual, casual . . . " I tell myself. There is a place called "The Small Cafe" near the University and when I am through teaching I meet her there for tea. This becomes a practice. The cafe has pink walls. She is wearing white one day, sitting across from me, and I notice that her nails are manicured, polished. When she picks up the tea cup her glossy, blunt nails tell me she is neither feminine nor masculine, but something else. And this is what I am attracted to—the other-worldliness of the true androgyne. I see time for hundreds and hundreds of years and this is the epitome of who she is: a woman who was an animal, who was a spirit, who was the earth, who was all—and I mark this moment, as I do all moments with her.

The cafe owner soon gets to know us and one day produces two silk scarves from France. Dorey takes her scarf and wraps it around my shoulders and then takes my scarf out of my hand and wraps it around herself and then says something coy and quick, like, "Now we are married."

One night Lisa and I are in bed. She is brushing her fingers across my neck, at my side. I am lulled and I choose this inane moment to tell her. I tell Lisa that I am seeing Dorey, that it is different between Dorey and me this time. "Dorey has given up on Ann. She wants to see me again," I say.

"Are you in love with her?" she asks.

"What difference does it make? I know I want to be with her."

"But do you love her?"

"Oh, I don't know." I am whiny. "What is love?" Maybe I am trying to be evasive, but maybe I believe that Dorey and I belong to a separate world and we believe that our love is not nearly so jubilant nor so mundane as the love between others and that we do not exist as women in love but rather, we exist to consume: consume the world and consume each other.

Lisa bolts up from the bed and stands against the wall. "I have heard all your Dorey stories. I will never believe it will be different, that it will work between you two. But I will leave you to find that out for yourself." She goes to the bathroom to vomit as she is genuinely ill. And for a while I speak to neither Dorey nor Lisa as the whole thing makes me ill, too.

And soon Lisa is packed. The UPS comes one drizzly morning to pick up the boxes. Her mother arrives to drive her to the airport. Lisa departs as I watch from the steps of our house. She is going to Arizona where it is warmer and where her father lives. Lisa and I bought the damn house together and I like the damn house but now I'm going to sell the damn house. I don't want to see it again.

I call Dorey to tell her that Lisa and I have broken up.

"OH?" she says.

"Yes," I say.

"I suppose that means we should see each other soon." She is too cool.

"Yeah," I say. We hang up with no date, no plans. Too cool. The two of us are so damned cool. And in the midst of this I am feeling alone, panicky. I try to remember how I felt with Dorey, how everything would be right. My heart sinks as I feel that nothing is right.

Dorey and I have a strange conversation where we agree that we will each be alone for a few months while we adjust. This only makes a little sense as I have just broken up with Lisa to be with her. So I move back home while I look for an apartment. One night, as I am sitting in the basement at my brother's old school desk, I feel a worm in my brain—large, and wet, twisting, nibbling at my brain tissue and killing me. The worm has been around in my body for some time. When I was nine it was in my legs, at twelve it was in my stomach, and at fifteen, my heart. Now it has inched its way upward to my brain. It laughs as it eats. It laughs at how helpless I am to get at it.

I equate Dorey to my worm. I feel it is beyond my control to stop something which may potentially devour me. It occurs to me that I wish to be devoured.

I call my friend Mar-Beth and I say, "You know I can feel it sometimes. I will be painting or I will be hunched over my typewriter and I can feel it. I feel that god damned worm. In my brain, eating it out."

And Mar-Beth, who is very cool, says, "Uh-huh. Well, Alexandra, maybe you feel life sweeping beyond you and you feel old in the face of death, already ruined so to speak, by all that we know in our psychoanalytic age."

"And what do we know?" I say.

"That society seeks to destroy itself."

"And to preserve itself."

"Yeah, that too. But mainly we're destroying ourselves."

And I say, "No, Mar-Beth, it's something else. Only some of us will be destroyed. I think this worm thing knows all about it."

At this she loses patience: "Alexandra. Stop it. You don't have a worm 'THING' in your brain!" It seems to be what I need to hear.

So I am home, living downstairs. This, because my old bedroom upstairs has been converted into a gym. When you open the door you see two treadmills. One for her, my mother, and one for him, my father. There's a built-in TV with VCR and some shelves where the family photo albums are kept. It has become the room of choice for my mother. She is there most of the time.

So one night I am downstairs dancing to old Diana Ross and the Supremes. I think if I dance fast enough then I won't feel the worm and I won't feel sick, sick about Dorey and the whole thing. I think if I keep moving I will forget. So I dance. I dance round to that old basement passageway which leads to my brother Stretch's old room. The basement is built for dancing. Shale flooring. My mother thought shale floors would turn it into a *Town and Country* home. There are also natural rock walls and waterfalls throughout the basement.

And I come upon Stretch's room, which is now used for storage. He used to have an aquarium filled with snails. We used to put the snails in our hands and thumb the smoothness of the shells while we talked. I turn on the lights thinking I can sit on the bed, but the bed is gone. Most of the space on the floor is taken up by the punch bowl.

I investigate the punch bowl and things around it. Towels, old coat hangers, baskets. I surmise that the punch bowl has been down there for at least a year.

I remember one of our holiday parties with the punch bowl. Someone was once there from *Town and Country* and they wrote it up. My mother stood next to the punch bowl in black dress, pearls, a broad smile. The blurb said, "The most fashionable and prestigious smiles in Chicago could be seen at Mr. and Mrs. Ted Brown's annual holiday affair . . ." After the *Town and Country* article everyone believed it— they believed all that about smiling and being prestigious and fashionable at the Browns'.

The holiday parties became a tradition. A place to be seen in Chicago. Everywhere, laughter everywhere—but especially in a circle around the punch bowl. By the end of the evening everyone by the punch bowl was pasty with shit-eating, gleaming grins.

I made a study of my father at one of the parties. It was during one Christmas vacation from college when I was feeling particularly ill towards the world and detached. He is a thin man. He limps as a result of an auto accident he had in his youth. But he has his moments of being the life of the party, organizing chug-a-lug games around the punch bowl.

He got the idea one year to pour the punch into the old silver beer steins that had been stored away for years. "Everyone!" he yelled. "Champagne by the stein!" The steins were promptly polished by a silent Mrs. Estevez. The punch was poured in. The steins went round the room. "We have a holiday look now," someone insisted. Punch dripped down chins and was sloshed on velvet dresses. The chef, the Mexican woman and I watched. My father was happy. He was beaming.

Seeing my dead stare, he shot me a glance across the room, it said: Don't you *dare* get moody here. Don't you DARE!

I remember . . . wearing jeans at these affairs

and standing at the rear of the room.

And at midnight, the women of the Christmas party stood everywhere with heads tilted back, chests bubbling out of their dresses, white dimples apparent there in cleavage and everywhere, laughter from their aging faces.

This is what I had come to see. By the end of the evening, these women had moved to the living room couches. The tree blinked from the corner with small Italian lights and the women were all leaned forward in chairs giving one unified whisper to the room. I sat in one of the chairs, struck with quiet. I was in love. I was in love with them all. Me, the quiet girl in jeans, wanted to be all women and all secrets between women.

At the end of the evening—I stood in the foyer with the door open and the snow blowing against my face, watching them fade down the steps, the women hobbling, tiredly leaning on dark-suited men and the men bracing themselves in the cold-dark night. Spurts of laughter arose from the hobbling figures. I watched them fade into cars that disappeared in the snow. I came in and found my mother and father laid out in the easy chairs.

Staring into the last burning embers of the fireplace they said, "Well, what do you kids think? Success?"

"It was great. It was fun," I, strangely, was the first to say, and then I came forward and kissed them each on the cheek. "I love you," I said to my mother. "I love you," I said to my father.

As I was going to my bedroom I heard her say, "I'm tired Ted, dead tired. I don't know if I could do this again next year. Thank the Lord I have Mrs.

Estevez coming tomorrow to help take down the tree."

"Evelynn," he said, "what are you talking about? Of course we'll do it next year. It's tradition here."

"You can keep your traditions; I'll keep mine," she said.

"You," he said. "I can't understand you."

The great roaring fire of the Christmas season usually burned itself out in this way.

For the longest time I wanted to be this: A party. I wanted to look for this: A party. I wanted to boil and sweat and be a cauldron and tip glasses with some good drunk people—to tip, to swish, to gulp and throw liquor way back in my mouth and have damn good conversations in spite of it. To be somebody, some drunken, brilliant somebody, and then go for more. That was what I wanted, to be like a flashing party. I wanted people to come to me and my party and we would have conversation so beautiful it would be like prayer. We would pray till three a.m., drunkenly, by a quiet fire. And when the streets were gleaming with rain, we would choose to take walks right then. And in my party at sunrise we would joke about it being sunset and go to sleep, heaped onto each other's gleaming naked bodies. I remember my father standing high on the table with his champagne steins in hand and with his party-congregation about him. It would be like that. It would be religious.

And this is what I think about as I am going to sleep that first night in the basement of my parents' house. I think that if I could have a dream come true then life would absorb me like a party.

I dream of Dorey. I spend the entire dream drunkenly staggering and holding out my hands like a cup. I am trying to catch Dorey's hair. But then I keep seeing her hair, like a black stream of water, running through my hands.

I call her one night with my parents asleep and all the lights off in the house. I sit on the floor of the basement. As soon as she answers I feel I have done the wrong thing.

And I ask her, "What the fuck am I doing living at home? I should be living with you!"

"Alexandra," she says. "You'll feel better in a week or two. I'm moving home myself."

"Why?" I ask. "It would be better if we just moved in together. It seems we're moving backwards instead of forwards."

"I have some thinking to do. Don't you want to think about us? What we'll be doing the rest of our lives?"

"No," I said. "I just want to get on with it and LIVE the rest of our lives."

"We can't now."

"Dorey, I've been hearing that from you for years and it kind of scares me to hear that now."

"I'm thinking of us," she says.

"Forget it, Dorey. I don't care," I say. We hang up. We agree to keep in touch or something, I don't remember. All I know is that I'll be calling her tomorrow in a panic and I don't know why.

One night, as I am living at home and waiting for Dorey to call, I decide to go to the bar called Nicole's, a quasi-chic lesbian scene, where the walls are made of glass block and the dance floor is slick, black and up high like a stage. And I buy a mineral water soda and sit there, legs crossed, on a bar stool against the wall . . . watching women and wondering what the fuck I am doing there when I'd rather be with Dorey.

"Can I help you with your drink?"

My drink is falling out of my hand. I don't know this until the woman with long cascading hair and thin legs in tight, near-white blue jeans, says this. And shyly (because I am shy at times) I say, "No, no thank you," and set the stupid bottle down on the bar.

And shyly (because it seems she is shy and I like this) she says, "I know you. I mean I don't know you. But I've seen you before."

"Really?" I ask.

She laughs (self-conscious, wonderful) and says, "Yes, it was at the Taste of Chicago Festival. I nearly came up to you then, but you were with someone else."

Somehow I get it across to her that I am not with

anyone now (maybe I am with Dorey but who knows). Anyway, I decide not to think about Dorey for the evening. She asks me to dance. Somehow we end up in her car and there is some slow shy kissing. And I want that. It is a release from Dorey.

It is not the same as Dorey, but I am instinctively, instantaneously in love with this other woman.

I suppose we share our shyness. She drives me home and quietly we start kissing. Lightly, she moves. I like her lips, large and sculpted, giving some exotic quality to her. I like her thin jeaned figure— leather jacket. Mostly I like her shyness, because she struggles with it, holding back and coming forward at the same time, so that in five minutes she is on top of me, straddling me, and then suddenly she is by the window with her fingers in her mouth, apologizing. I tell her not to apologize. I understand it completely.

It is a dreary day. It is winter. It snows. It is January. Days fade grayly and coldly one into the next. I sit on my bed in the downstairs family room. I feel a reprieve. I pretend the bed, in its white sheets, is like a beach. It is an island beach in the middle of the ocean. From my bed that is like a beach I can see pictures of a grandfather I never knew. He is framed, and set on the highboy. Old album covers of Diana Ross & the Supremes are scattered on an old cocktail table. I have the old stereo cranked. Diana Ross's voice sounds as if it is coming from static blue heavens. And under the covers I feel as if I am taking a swim in the deep ocean. I love being underwater. Yes, I really do. I love being alone sometimes and feeling like I am under water . . .

I decide that I don't know what the hell I am doing with Dorey, so I call her. "It is too soon," she says.

"Too soon for what?" I ask.

"Alexandra, you're being stupid on purpose."

"I'm not," I charge back.

"Look," she says. "If it happens, it'll happen. We have to trust that it is meant to be. Forcing it won't work."

"I don't want to force it. I just want it to happen."

"I still have some things to work out."

"Like what?"

Then she says it. "You can date other women if you want. I'm just not ready."

Then I say it. "Well, fuck you, you know. 'Cause I am seeing someone else," I say. "As a matter of fact, I am."

She hangs up on me. I expected it.

I have a date this evening, with her, the shy one. Her name is Diana. She knows about Dorey. I told her about Dorey and how I was thinking of Dorey a lot and all— but how I wanted it to stop. Stop soon. I just didn't know how to stop it. I don't know. She just listened.

"I like you," I said at the end of the phone conversation. It came out like lead. Stupid.

"Thank-you," she said. "I like you too."

It's true, I like Diana. I get ready for my date. I put on Diana Ross and begin to put on clothes, take them off, put on some others I like more. Then I sit down for a while. I click on the old console TV against the wall. *Rio Grande* is on. I turn the volume off.

The dog comes by as I'm sitting there. I pet his head. "Old Star," I say, "old king of the doggies." I say this out of habit— it seems to calm me. He lies at the foot of the bed, groans, looks up at me, and falls asleep. I pretend that the dog is on the shoreline and I am on the beach. I pretend that it is only us two left in the world, and really, it comes down to this: The dog and I understand each other.

Though I am determined to think of nothing, I end up thinking of Dorey.

I feel deathly ill at the thought of trying to analyze it. But I do anyway: "We're not speaking," I say to myself and to the dog. "We're supposed to be giving each other some room right now. To acclimate. But sometimes I think this is the way it's supposed to be. I'm really not supposed to be with her and she's not supposed to be with me. We're only supposed to be saving ourselves for each other. The idea is to keep things nebulous, ethereal, unreal. If things weren't so nebulous we wouldn't be so lost trying to define them. The whole idea is to stay lost."

The dog stays asleep, but seems to understand because when I look at his face he looks sad. "The game gets tiring," I continue. "God damn right, it gets tiring. How long have I known her anyway? One year? And then there were the two years I spent with

Lisa in between. So that makes a total of three years! God, I can't believe it myself sometimes. Three years! It gets depressing." I pat his head philosophically and get dressed.

I remember . . . Mar-Beth and I on the beach. It was at the new beach in Winnetka, we could see all the highrises of Chicago far off, but close in, it was quiet. We were sixteen, with eyes closed, listening to the waves and to the birds and to each other. I asked, "Mar-Beth . . . what do you think your life will be? I mean, when you get older, what do you expect to accomplish?"

Mar-Beth got up and knelt on the blanket and held her arms up to the sky and said, "You know, I think sometimes of what I will accomplish in life . . . and I think I will have a few good friends in life . . . and we will get fabulously drunk some nights . . . and feel our friendship as intensely . . . as intensely as the borealis lights the night; as intensely as the sun heats this day, we will feel that bond of friendship as intensely as anything that has ever lived has ever felt— and what's more we will all know it and look at each other drunkenly upon the moment of knowing— and that will be that. She looked at me cock-eyed, "A few good friends, you know?"

I sit on my bed. *Rio Grande* is still on TV. The Texas skies are powder blue in *Rio Grande*.

I begin to daydream of Dorey. She teases me by

walking naked across a Texas road. I am in the silver
Cadillac. I have come to a dead stop in order to avoid
hitting her and her naked body. I am furious when
she walks on to a dry field of flowers. I could have
killed her, doesn't she know that? I scream to her, "I
could have killed you. You! Hey You! Woman! I could
have killed you, don't you care?" She looks at me like
I'm crazy, and I feel crazy, blood pumping and all, as
I get out of the car, slam the door and follow her.

Cars are passing outside slow in the snow, while
I lie on the bed, thinking of her.
Then I hear the rattling. A loud rattling. Un-
nerving. Our metal spiral staircase. The spiral
staircase had been quite a hit at cocktail parties.
Couples would navigate down it, drunkenly.
It is my mother. Her diamond rings scrape the
rail. I see her coming down, slippers first, then the
green robe. She stops at that half-way point, the
midway step. She always stops on this step. In my
entire life, I don't think I've seen my mother actually
come into our basement.
From my beach position, I can see her green
robe shimmer. She bends over to talk.
"So quiet," she says. "Why so quiet?" I see her
face. Prominent taut cheeks, and gold flash in her
hazel eyes. As soon as she appears we are in the
throes of some intense emotion, which will lead to
confrontation and then to the acquiescing of one to
the other. It always does.
"What's going on down here?" she asks.
I want to say: Nothing in the world is going on

down here. Largely, grandly, nothing in the world is going on down here. You know that. Why are you asking? So that you can create the intimacy of wanting to know—and then disappear, before you actually know?

"I don't know, was I quiet?" I ask from my bed in the corner of the basement. I want to tell her of Dorey. But then that would have to be another mother, another life.

"I was upstairs and I didn't hear a sound. Is something wrong?"

"No. Nothing's wrong. I was just getting dressed."

"Oh, were you?"

For a minute I don't know what else to say and am afraid that always, I will not know what to say to her.

"Where are you going?" She sways . . . the stairs groan. She looks majestic in the green robe.

"Out," I say. "I'm going out. With someone. Diana. You don't know her. I don't think you know her. I just met her."

She is quiet. She understands everything and chooses not to know anything all in the same moment. She knows that I am in love with women. I've told her/them. Even when they didn't want to know, I told them. A thousand different ways I have told them I am a lesbian including, "I am a lesbian"–a thousand different ways they have told me they don't want to hear it. She really doesn't want to know. Ditto for my father. Words have never been this family's strong point anyway.

We don't even look at each other. My stare is on the bead of her slippers. I am curious about my mother. She is a woman who is too much. Perversely

I feel it come upon me, my desire to please her.

I explain that Diana is a new acquaintance. She lives in the suburbs and works in a bicycle factory. That is all I know for now.

My mother for some reason is suddenly in despair, probably because I'm gay and worse yet, going out with someone who works in a bicycle factory. So she says: "Oh, Alexandra. No! You're going out to the suburbs in all this snow! Don't be silly."

"I'm not being silly."

"You are," she says.

"God damn it, I'm not being silly! I'm going out tonight." And then I walk back to the mahogany framed mirror in the back of the basement. I lie on my bed that is a beach. I am silent. This works very well. She gets up. The green of her robe flashes. She disappears up the staircase. First the robe disappears, then the slippers. It is the Ascension. At the top of the staircase she stops and calls down, "Your father and I are going to Betty's wake tonight. Are you coming?"

Betty Reese was a woman who made herself famous at cocktail parties by wearing blue satin dresses, out of which sprung operatic breasts. She was lovely. I had this theory, that she too was a woman who was too much, and that she probably died because of it. Just burned herself out—like a shooting star. It was probably that combination of Slavic breasts, children, beauty, and knowledge—that killed her. Everyone at cocktail parties would stumble towards her and confide all secrets to her. By the end of the evening every man became a boy in front of her; and every woman, more of a woman. Now she was dead. I was sure, far off, part of the world had collapsed with her.

"No," I say. "I don't want to go to the wake."

"Why aren't you going to wakes?" she asks. Persistent.

"I don't know."

"Why aren't you going to wakes?" she reiterates. "You didn't go to Tim's wake either."

Tim was our neighbor. I guess he was a drunk, though nobody called him that. When he died his landlord put the contents of his townhouse in the yard. It didn't seem right to expose him that way. I mean, there was a bent bird cage there, with seed and shit in it, and lots of old newspapers and old beer cartons. And all along we had thought he was someone grand, the way he walked around the neighborhood with his suit on all the time. And so I didn't think I was going to find out who he was by going to his wake or anything. I thought it was better just to leave it all alone.

"I didn't go to Tim's wake because I was ill," I reply.

"Alex," she says, "you don't have to lie." There is a pause between us. "You should go to the wake. It helps to bring the death home," she says. "It was immature not to go to Tim's funeral and to think that you could avoid something by not going."

"Please just leave it," I say. I am staring at the ceiling, lying on my beach bed staring at the ceiling, hoping I will hear her leave soon.

"All right, if you change your mind, let us know."

Thank god.

I am dressed. I go upstairs with my coat on, and a huge fur hat which was her Christmas gift to me last year.

"Come say good-bye," she says from the bathroom. She is at the vanity staring in the mirror. I kiss her on the cheek. I see on the counter all her make-up, her perfume, the compilation of what is her. I am afraid that she is going to die soon, too. And I think I am crazy for always thinking this. I wish I could stop; but it's like saying I wish I could stop the world. "I love you," I say.

"Be careful in that snow," she says. And shaking her head while she applies mascara she says, "I don't know why you're going. It's no thing to do on a night like this. Take a blanket from the closet for your car."

On my way out my father walks in. He has a black suit on. He seems taller, more serious. I notice his limp. Some days when I see him I forget that he limps. I forget all about it until in my sleep I say, "That's right. He limps."

And it makes me think that he is going to die soon, too. I can feel it. I kiss him good-bye hoping to get past him quickly. His face is beet red from the cold. "Weren't you coming tonight?" he says as we both stand in the entryway for an eternity with the snow drifting in, blowing around our feet.

"No, but I love you," I say and quickly walk past him. He calls after me, then shuts the door. After the door is shut I can hear him yell for my mother.

In the car all I can think of is getting to Diana's. Once I am there I will release myself.

Diana's mother peers first through a crack in the door.

I see two round eyes, burnished orange hair. Then she stands back just far enough so I can get in. We are face to face. Nose to nose practically.

"Diana will be down in a minute," she says. A wooden spoon is in her hand. I want to take the spoon gently from her and watch her try to get it.

"The weather is terrible," the mother says to me. She backs up. Her back is to the cheap molding of the foyer.

"It was awful," I answer.

After a moment's pause she stares at me blankly and says, "How long did it take you to get here?"

Luckily, at this moment, I see Diana on the steps. She has the jeans on. The same white and torn jeans of the night I met her, a simple white blouse that just reveals small breasts behind it. "You've met my mother," she says. The mother nods at me. Then we fly up to her room.

There is a white wicker bed, with canopy.

I do not have time to assess if Diana is a mystery or not.

Quickly the room blurs and the canopy creaks and we are slowly tossing ourselves around. Diana, at one point, is on top of me, biting my ear, telling me I am late. "Your mother kept me at the door," I whisper. "I had to talk with her. It would have been uncivil of me just to rush up here, wouldn't it?"

"No, it wouldn't have," she says and bites my ear again. We wrestle and stop, breathless, on our knees under the canopy. I stare into the darkness between her legs.

She catches my stare and unzips her pants. I

unzip mine.

She unbuttons her blouse. I take off my sweater. My breasts hang naked. I am embarrassed for half a second, until she reaches over and lets her fingers brush past my nipples.

She takes off her blouse, her bra, and kneeling there, I feel I am praying to her. We are silent.

The rising and falling of her breasts is hypnotic and then things happen, sort of slow and fast at the same time. She works off my jeans and then suddenly she is going down on me so calmly and exquisitely that I want to beg for an ending to it. Shit, I am nearly dying.

Suddenly, she stops. I catch my breath.

She is breathing heavily. "I can't," she whispers.

"Can't what?" I ask.

"I can't finish this."

"Shit." I move away. I begin to eye my pants, my sweater . . . "What?" I ask. "Can't finish what?" I know it is a stupid question but I am stalling for time.

"I mean I can't do it . . . be intimate, if you're not sure of me."

"But I don't know you."

"But you are sure of her."

"Her, oh, HER. Does SHE have to come into this?"

"Yes, I mean . . . Well, maybe I'm jealous or something."

"Shit, just forget her, will you?"

"You haven't," she says.

"Maybe I haven't. But I want to."

"Not through me."

"Jesus, why not?"

She looks hurt.

"I'm sorry," I say. "I don't know. Sometimes you try to forget about someone by going out with someone else, don't you? It works sometimes, doesn't it? And you know . . . sometimes you end up with the new person . . . you can . . . it happens that way . . . "

She moves away.

"Shit."

"Shit, yeah, shit," she says and gets up to find her blouse.

"Well, shit if I'm going to lie here naked while you're getting dressed," I say because I don't know what else to say. And find my own clothes, slip them on quickly and sit on the bed again.

She takes my hand. I look at her. I am silent.

"I'm sorry," I say again. "I'm always saying that to people, you know? But it's true. I didn't mean to take advantage or anything."

"I know," she answers.

I notice she is looking down to her blouse, which is open, down to her breasts. She studies her nipples for half a second, hard under her cotton blouse. I like her for that moment. Maybe I love her.

I take her cheek and kiss it and kneel down in front of her, kissing her breasts and nuzzling my head between her legs.

I unzip the pants she has just zipped up and put my hand where it is warm. I stand up and take the hair she has just combed and I run my fingers through it soft-like, and then, I don't know, we end up making love.

I do not stay. She does not ask me to stay. I get back in my car in six inches of snow to drive back to the city.

I get home at three a.m. My father's wallet is on the counter. My mother's fur coat is hanging in the bathroom to air. Before I go to sleep I call old Star to the bed and I explain to him that when you're in love with somebody, and when only that one person in the world can understand who you are and why you do things, it leaves you very lonely sometimes.

The next afternoon, at an Indian restaurant with walls covered in blood-red wallpaper, Mar-Beth sits across from me shaking paprika onto her chicken curry. She is humming as she does it.

"I have a pressing thought," I say.

"Well?" She pauses, paprika shaker in hand.

"Perhaps it is only arbitrary that we live, since we will all die. And then only arbitrary that we die."

Mar-Beth stares at the ceiling lights. "Look for the well-spring, dear," she says half-mockingly. "You must. Because life is hard and flawed, and dying is perfect. So you must look for that life which will transcend the perfect, blissful, assuaging nature of death."

The next day is Betty Reese's funeral and I go because suddenly it makes sense to go to a funeral.

Exhausted relatives in black fill the parlor chairs.

My father comes up to me. He looks thin in his black suit. I keep thinking I don't know him. I keep thinking we missed some great talk.

He speaks to me in a voice that seems unnaturally loud. "We're glad you came," he says. There is industrial grey carpeting in the room and my eyes are on the edges of the steel grey casket. "Byron calls it the dreamless sleep," he says. In saying this he has created the smallest dot on the face of the earth signifying where the lines of both our paths have crossed. He quickly changes the subject. "Did you get a ride here? Will you need a ride in the procession? You can ride with your mother and me."

"I have a ride," I say.

"Ride with your mother anyway. I'll have to go soon," he says. "I have some business at the office."

"So then you're *not* riding?" I say to clarify.

"No." He looks stiff and pale. "No, I have some business at the office."

Then panic sweeps over him. I know he is suddenly filled with panic because we are of the same species. His eyes dart about the room. He prepares for flight. He scratches his palm. He eyes the doorway. "Your mother's over there," he says.

And then he is gone. Like the Lone fucking Ranger.

I walk over to my mother. She is absently winding strands of pearls around her fingers. She has painted her fingernails white. She wears black eyeliner. She looks elegant, waxing. On close examination it occurs to me that she could look grotesque. It is the combination of the pearls, the white nail polish, and the purple scarf in her hair. Mar-Beth says that sometimes the quirks of people pop out just like the stuffing in an overstuffed couch. If I blinked my eyes I could see a grotesqueness to her.   And if I blinked my eyes again she would look elegant.

"Tammy was asking about you earlier," she says.

"Tammy?"

"Betty's girl. She has a boyfriend."

"Yeah?"

"You should speak to Tammy. Your friendship meant a lot to her."

I see Tammy standing with her boyfriend across the hall from me. I remember Tammy dancing in the breezeway with skinny knees and skinny arms.

"Tammy, hi. Alexandra, remember?" I take her hand lightly. She smiles stiffly and keeps smiling. There seem to be waves of smiles coming toward me.

She asks if I remember the breezeway.

I remember . . . playing Herman's Hermits and "spotlight" dancing on top of the radiator covers.

There are awkward pauses between our remembrances. She introduces me to the man in black corduroys. Britz is his name. He is a car mechanic. She has a condo in the suburbs now. They will live there right after they are married, while they look for a house. I tell her it sounds nice. It occurs to me that they make a handsome couple.

Later I go up to view Betty Reese and what I think, is that she should have lived longer.

Later at the grave site, Tammy has thrown herself into her mother's grave. She is down there in the dirt hole. She is screaming for her mother not to go away. Her thin arms are thrown around the casket, embracing it. The funeral guests stand in a circle, on the crusty cold earth, horrified at the girl in the grave.

Britz runs up and lies on the dirt alongside the hole and reaches down with one arm to pull her out. He ushers her away from the grave site towards the waiting car. They are beautiful. This is what I think. For a moment I am in love with Tammy again or perhaps in love with both of them. I am in love with the way some people continually confront death with these small demonstrations of life.

For days I want to be like them. I think of them. I think of Britz and Tammy confronting the loss. And I try to put my finger on it: What great loss is it, what is it that I feel that only Dorey and I can confront in the world—just the loss of having loved and lost? Just that? Everyone feels that, don't they?

And so any day I expect Dorey to come knocking at my door and we will create a huge explosion as we step out into the world together. Dorey does not call. I am trapped in myself.

I think of Diana. There is a simplicity about her—not the drama that Dorey has—I am attracted to this, too. Still, I don't call her.

Instead, one night, I wander into Nicole's in search of Dorey. It is some sort of anniversary at Nicole's. Women in tux shirts go around serving little frankfurters on little sticks. They keep playing those slow songs. I keep wishing Dorey were there to dance with me.

Then I see Dorey come in. Right there, at the door. I see her before she sees me. I don't know why she stuns me, but she does. She sends quiet right to my heart. Her dark hair is pulled down in front of her eyes. She looks moody. She wears white: a huge white jacket and white baggy pants, and a white shirt buttoned to the neck. There is a rhinestone pin in the collar just below her chin. It flashes in the light.

I wave and feel stupid for one second until she comes over.

She wavers in front of me. She has been drinking. "Do you know what?" she says drunkenly. "I like the way you're dressed. I always liked the way you dress." I'm wearing a black outfit with white lipstick and rhinestone earrings. Then she adds, "Ann's working at Lord and Taylor. It was her dream, you know."

I am silent.

"She worked so hard to get that job."

Then I say, "Fuck, Dorey. We're talking about Ann now? I mean we haven't seen each other in weeks and when I saw you just now all I could think was that I loved you. Don't you want to come over and just tell me you love me or something? Can't it ever be simple? I mean I think we sabotage every meeting just so that we can build it up again."

"Shhhhh," she says and slides her arms around me. "Shhhhh. I love you."

"AAAAND?" I ask, searching for more assurance.

"And I love you, don't you know that?"

"More?"

"More what?" she asks flatly.

"Shit, Dorey." I say gathering my anger. "Shit. You haven't returned my calls. I wrote. You didn't write back. How the FUCK am I supposed to know that you love me?"

She begins to walk away and I grab her before all is lost. I want to stop the fight. I want to lose myself. "It's just that . . . Jesus, Dorey, sometimes you make me feel like an idiot for being in love with you!"

"OK, please. Let's stop. Let's just stop it now. I love you. I love YOU. You know that? I wouldn't say that to just anyone."

"What do you mean?" I ask.

"What do you mean, what do I mean?"

"I mean, why can't you just say 'I love you.' Why do you have to tell me you don't say it to 'just anyone,' as if I should be thankful."

"You make me despair sometimes," she says and she walks away.

I pull at her sleeve again and she comes back.

"I'm sorry," I say. "Let's dance. Let's just do something. Let's not argue."

She drags me into a corner. There, we dance, far away from the crowd on the dance floor. "I love you," she whispers.

"I love you, too," I say. "Dorey, we need to be together. Now, please. Together now and forever."

She puts her hand over my mouth. She tells me to be quiet. With her fingers still in my mouth, she kisses me. She pries my mouth open with her fingers and plays with her tongue going around my tongue. "I've missed you. I've been lying around dead and depressed thinking of you. It just scares me sometimes. Doesn't it scare you?"

"What?"

"Being together."

"Yeah."

We dance. We stumble through three other women's bars that evening. We stumble out of the last one, uproarious.

Then in the car there is silence. I think we are in love. Or perhaps we are angry. I can never tell.

It is 5:05 on Broadway. It is sunrise and I have pulled over into a cement and gravel parking lot so that Dorey can piss. She is crouched in that space between door and car. There is a bank in front of us. I stare at the bank clock. It's an odd time to get giddy but I am standing in the middle of the lot, drunk, thinking about how much I love life and how Dorey and I will take it by storm. I keep my eye on the clock, just to mark the moment. The sky is cracked with pink. Glorious. Suddenly I see Dorey walking toward the glass walls of the bank.

"Dorey," I call.

"I am walking into this glass wall and I believe it will move for me. God says if you believe, you can move mountains."

I catch her as she slams into the wall. When she turns there is blood spouting from her nose. There is a long thin gash in her forehead and blood oozes from that. Lines of blood run down her face. "It looks worse than it is, I know," she says holding out a hand to catch the blood falling from her chin. A small pool has collected around the collar of the white shirt. Blood seeps between the rhinestones of her pin, making it seem grotesque and alive.

I take hold of her arm, pulling her to the car.

"God has lied," she says gallantly and pushes me away with her one unbloodied hand.

"Are you hurt?" I ask and try to hold her, maybe the same way Britz held Tammy.

"No, I'm fine," she says, pushing me away again and stumbling toward the car.

"Fuck you," I say.

I walk toward the car, not really with her, but more like alongside her. She sways heavily, drunkenly. And finally she leans on the hood waiting for me to open the car door. Blood splashes on the car and stains every piece of her white clothing. I take my blanket out of the car and wrap her in it but she really doesn't let me do this. She takes it from me and hurriedly tries to wrap herself, then hurriedly gives up, so that the blanket hangs off her like a sloppy toga. And then she gets in the car, slamming the door on the blanket so that I now know that the tail end of it is out there, on the cement. I decide to let the blanket hang out.

In the car I wipe at her blood with the ends of the blanket.

She yanks the rear view mirror her way. "I know," she says, studying her face. "I know it's not as bad as it looks because I don't feel a thing."

I push with my hands at the blood smears left on her cheek.

She pushes back at me.

"Stop it god damn it. I'm trying to help."

"I'm trying to help," she imitates me.

"You're a fucker."

"I'm a fucker."

"Shut up."

"OK, I'll shut up."

I wrap her more tightly in the blanket.

"Why must I always be weaker than you?" she asks.

"You are stronger," I say.

"Bullshit."

"Shut up. I think you need stitches. Maybe you have a concussion. I'm taking you to a hospital."

She sits bolt upright. "I'm not going to a hospital," she says. She squirms to get her arms out of the blanket. She sits there with her fists clenched saying, "I'll die before you take me to a hospital."

We argue more about the hospital but then she gets sick and hangs her head out the window and vomits on the outside of my car. I am silent. I can only look at her smeared with vomit and blood. "Jesus, you're pathetic," I say.

"Don't say that," she says and now she is crying.

"Jesus, I'm sorry. I didn't mean it."

"Doesn't matter. It's true."

"Oh, fuck it all, Dorey. We need each other right now."

She touches at my hand as if agreeing. "Just tell me where the fuck you want to go," I say softly.

"Home."

So I drive her home. The sky is pearled pink. The first rays of sun shoot across the tops of houses and she is oddly beautiful as she gets out of the car. A crusty scab is forming on the bridge of her nose. The blanket is still half-wrapped around her. The tails of it drag on the cement as she stumbles away.

"Call me later," I yell.

"I will," she says, and I know she won't.

I call Dorey a few days later and I don't know what to say to her. She is quiet. Uncomfortable. I hold the phone in my hand, looking at it as I lie on my bed in the dark.

"Is Ann around?" I ask.

"What a way to start a conversation."

"Is she there?" I ask again because I am nervous.

"Who?"

"Fuck, who do you think? Ann. Is she there with you? Have you been spending time with her?"

"Alexandra, I can't talk now. I'm ill. Believe what you want." She hangs up.

That's it. I've had it. I've had it. Lent is coming. I make up my mind to give Dorey up. I sit on my bed that is like a beach. I read a book by Salinger. Dorey gave it to me. She had underscored all kinds of passages from Salinger. One was about two girls from a posh summer resort; they were mundane, their summer was boring, but one girl could be counted on for always bringing a fresh can of tennis balls to the country club. Dorey had written in the margins there, "I'd rather die." Then there was another story about a young couple, good-looking, just starting out, on their honeymoon and all, but she's in the hotel room talking to her mother about how her husband seems depressed; while he's out on the beach talking to a little girl, making friends with her, making up names for fish and all that, and it seems the little girl might understand him better than his wife. In the end he commits suicide. In the margin Dorey had written, "That's what it's like out there. Salinger is so perfect in capturing it."

I thought that Dorey and I were like that. It seemed we could capture all the pain and insensitivity of nature that eluded everyone else.

47

I sleep for days. I wake and read Salinger. I fall back asleep. I long for sleep, like a drug. Women fill my dreams. I am afraid sometimes that I am lost in these dreams, that my life is wasted in this dream. But then in the dream everything seems right and nothing is wasted.

I call Dorey again. It is a month after she walked into the glass wall. Snow is beginning to melt. The ground is soft and musty smelling. And I have renewed hope. We get together because it is her birthday. I am dressed in black—which means black pumps and black pants and a black blouse, open, and eyes rimmed in black pencil. And she is wearing silver pants and a blue jacket and patent leather pumps and we are oh so fashionable and feel oh so much on the cutting edge of life. Yet we barely kiss in the car. We touch each other's backs or something. And at the restaurant with three gay waiters around us we fall more into our element. We feed each other the small veal rolls that come on our plates and we order wine which comes in a silver bucket. The man who brings it tells us he has never seen two better looking women together. It is a small compliment, slightly vulgar if you think about it, but we needed it, to perpetuate the myth of who we were.

She smiles, wickedly, takes my hand to her lips and kisses it. She asks me to come to the bathroom where she will fuck me. I respond no, but for some inexplicable reason find myself excited.

And I do ask myself sometimes. I do ask myself what this is all about.

She takes a pen and writes on my wrist, "You blew it." She puts the pen down. She drinks her wine. The waiter who thinks we are good looking now brings us a bottle of champagne, compliments of the house.

"Why did you write that?" I ask.

"I knew you would ask," she says. "You always ruin things by asking about them. It's typical of you."

"Shit, you know. Just shit."

She sees I'm upset, that the evening is about to go sour on us. She rescues it. "I don't know. Don't worry. It has nothing to do with you. I'm crazy. Just remember that. Here, give me your arm."

I show her my arm again.

She dabs her napkin in the champagne. "That's why they brought this here," she says as she dabs and wipes at my wrist with the napkin.

When she is finished I am silent.

"Now we'll go home," she says

We pay the bill. She ushers me out the door, to the car. She puts my head in her lap as she drives. She sort of pets my head. She pulls at my hair, surrounds my neck with her large hands. My head is buried in her thighs. Because she is wearing pants, I can't get to her skin. That is OK. I find myself licking the cotton of her pants.

The next week I finally find an apartment and move out of my temporary quarters at home. I invite Dorey over.

"Very nice," she says as she walks through. I have painted the dining room and the living room a sort of ballroom red. It could be grotesque, or it could be romantic, depending on how one looks at it. There are mirrors all over the "ballrooms." And I've hung old-fashioned heavy curtains everywhere. She looks good in it. Who knows. Maybe I bought everything with her in mind.

"Romantic. It's a place to make love," she says, and sits down on the black couch I've had covered in chintz.

Some opera music is on the stereo. She moves to a Louis XIV chair. It is stiff-backed and I stand behind her, massaging her neck. "We should talk," I say.

"Not now," she says. She gets up and kneels on the chair. I stand back a bit and she falls forward, trying to kiss me. Only the back of the chair keeps her from tumbling forward. We kiss. We kiss again. I tell her to stay there while I draw the shades on the window. I tell her she is a choir boy and we are in church. We make religious love right there on the living room floor.

She calls two weeks later. There is no mention of our previous lovemaking. I ask her over again. She comes up the back steps silently. She stands in the doorway with her Russian boots and hat on. Her skin is white, luminescent. Later, her coat is off, and in boots and hat, she stands in the middle of my bedroom, right where the streetlight comes in, and I wonder if she knows how beautiful she looks. I take off her blouse, I roll her pants down to the floor. I think, "Oh you, oh you in your Russian get-up. You know what you're doing to me. You know exactly what you're doing." But it's fleeting. She kisses me. We make serious love.

So the next weekend I rent a cabin in the snow. Always this plan: that soon she will see, as I see, that we are perfect in our bond to each other. Soon she will know, as I know, that our physical bond is everything. It is spiritual, intellectual, emotional. She will see our moments as I see our moments, as something etched and fine and immortal. And once she sees that they are perfect and beautiful she will dwell on them, save them, love them, as I do. She will come to me to create more moments. It will take the two of us to create these perfect moments. In this conspiracy we will belong to each other.

The cabin is located in the only nest of hills in Illinois. It is near the top of a ravine which is thawing with spring snow. The keys are behind the cast iron skillet as the proprietress said they would be.

We drink in our cabin. There is a wood bed with five Indian blankets piled upon it and a wood table sitting to the side. We lie on the couch with dinner in front of us. Our soup is long cold. The wine bottle is open. We wear socks and no clothes, as we are curled under a blanket. A fire roars in the large pot-bellied stove in the corner of the room. She looks particularly possessed. Her eyes are coal dark. Her hair is hanging in her face. Her skin, like the nights when any beast comes to the door in the snow, is white and gleaming. We consume glass upon glass of wine. She makes hearty, ridiculous toasts. She toasts to her father in the north of France whom she now imagines in his warm bathtub with his wife attending him. "He never loved me," she says. "Or he loves me but can't express it. He gives all his attention to Eleanor, his wife. She takes care of him, you know. Through all his strokes and operations. She takes care of him, not me. So he loves her, not me. He divides it like that. Some people can do that: divvy their love up like stock."

Finally she says, "To our strange life. To this strange woman who desires me. I find her strange in this desire, but it is entirely mine. You are mine and I am yours. We have lots to drink to," she says, and I really can't tell if she is being sarcastic or not. I go along with it.

"Dorey," I say. "I love you."

"Shhh. Shhh. Shhh," she says drunkenly. "I know that. Of course I do. Now shhhhh. Don't think," she says. "You drive me crazy when you think of it so much."

"Dorey," I say patiently. "I have to think. Someone has to think for us. If I don't think about us, who will?"

"You always underestimate me," she says. "It makes me sad. I have been thinking. I think all the time of you."

"What do you think?" I ask.

"I think it'll work," she says.

"You do?"

"Yes. Now, shhhh."

After a pause she says to me. "Do you know where he is now?"

"Who?" I ask.

"Father. My father. He is sitting in a small dark

kitchen." She points to our stove. "There is a little table, and a stove like this. The table is set up neatly with china and linen. It kills me that he has never asked me there. Only sent me pictures. I should hate him, but I don't."

"Forget him, Dorey. Your mother loves you."

"My mother's a drunk."

"But at least her love is there."

"It's conditional love."

"I love you," I say. "I love you."

We are both naked in bed and silently drawing pictures on each other with our hands. Dorey suddenly gets up and brings back our coats and boots. "We need enough firewood for the night." I begin to dress. "No, no, no," she says. "Just put this on." She hands me my coat. "And this. She hands me my boots. "That's all," she says and sits down on the bed to put her own boots on. And when we are standing with boots and coats on at the door, we stare at each other. Just stare for a long time and then we go out.

My coat is an old leather coat with fur lining and it feels luxurious on my skin. Shivers go up my legs but then suddenly I am warm and I crane my neck back to look at about a thousand stars in the sky. Slivers of her white legs now and then appear through the slit of her coat. We walk around the cabin and down the ravine, collecting scraps of wood as we go.

We find there are extra casks of wine hidden in the dirt behind the cabin. We unearth them. "Price tags," she says. "Are there supposed to be price tags on wine buried in the ground? What a downer. Always a reminder that someone else has been there before you."

"How much?" I ask, staring at the bottles in her hand.

"Thirty-six dollars apiece."

"Should we drink it?" I ask.

"You're so moral. It kills me. It does sometimes."

I kick at the snow trying to think of a good reason not to drink the wine. "It's not ours," I say.

"Go and get the corkscrew," she says. I go get the corkscrew. We sit in the snow and drink as a half-moon rises. My legs feel the cold earth underneath my coat and yet I am burning with warmth.

Drunkenly we gather our wood and return to our cabin. We leave one empty bottle of wine in the snow. We stuff kindling, newspaper, wood into the stove. We light it, shut the stove doors. Our coats and boots are left on the floor. The wine bottle we bring into the bed with us becomes uncorked and spills out. "The wine is going to stain the mattress," I say. "We'll get charged for it."

"You worry too much," she says, stopping her lovemaking to set the bottle upright on the table near the bed. She looks at me for the longest time. We are loaded with things we can't say. It ends there. She collapses on her side. We fall asleep.

In the middle of the night there is an explosion. Fire and logs soar from the belly of the stove. One log writhes and sizzles on the floor in its flame and heat. It seems like an animal, wounded, deformed. Dorey gets up and walks barefoot across the floor. I put on my boots and call for her to leave it. She doesn't hear.

54

She never hears when she doesn't want to. She crouches by the writhing log, her feet near the cinders. She is naked and she stares and I have half a second to think she is beautiful in the red glow of the flame. I am mesmerized by the pink glow of her skin.

She touches the log with her finger, then silently and slowly she flattens her palms to the charred surface and grasps the searing object in her hand, and stands up with it. She looks supernatural to me. She carries it back to the stove and heaves it into the fire. Her loins, her stomach, her breasts glow in the white/orange flames. And then I see her hands are charred black at the palms. There are red welts and blisters and curdled skin. And there is blood. "I am afflicted," she says, "and now you know it." Blood seeps from her bruised skin. She kneels down in front of me with her head in my lap. I hold her hands and stare at them. I had almost believed that she could do it— I had almost believed that she could pick up that god damned log and not get burned.

I whisper to her, "Dorey, Dorey, what are you doing to us? Damn you, Dorey! You idiot! You god damned idiot! You did it. You god damned idiot!"

"That's what they said about Christ," she mumbles. "They called him the idiot. Read it. It's in the Bible."

"You're a bigger idiot than Christ. Now are you happy?"

She laughs and then begins to cry. "Why do we have to be god to each other? Why does it have to be so much with you? I can't live up to it. Can't you see?"

"I didn't know," I say. "I didn't know I was asking it."

I don't know if water is right, but I take her to the basin and wash her hands. She is silent as I dab at the juices rising out of her palms. Then I take her to the bed and I rip the old T-shirt I brought from home, and wrap her hands in it. It occurs to me that she is naked, that I am bandaging her, that the two of us are quiet and naked in the room. She says to me, "You are studying me even now."

"Shut up. Just shut up." I say. I hug her gently. She hugs back. I unwrap her hands. "Wrapping is probably wrong. Jesus, Dorey, just hold them out in front of you. Don't touch anything. Burns get infected easily." Her hands were huge, swollen to twice their size.

We find a small hospital. They do a professional job on her hands. When we leave they are bandaged. They give her the name of a doctor in Chicago and some ointment. We drive back to the City in silence. She tells me that she will need time to heal. Her mother will take care of her. She will call me in two weeks.

My blood boils with anger. "I'm not leaving. I'm not leaving until you tell me why you just did that."

"I don't know," she says laconically.

"You *do* know!"

"I hate you. You and your analyzing. I'm ill now. Please. Leave. I want to be left alone. Can't you see I'm not feeling well. I need time to heal."

"I'm leaving. But Dorey, I *don't* know. I don't know you. Sometimes I think you do these things on purpose, just to put some crisis in our life."

"That's not true. I'm just being myself. I can't be any other way."

"I can't believe that," I say.

"That's because you believe what you want to believe about me. You always have."

"OK. I do," I say and am about to say more but she puts her bandaged hands to my lips and says, "No more today, please."

"Where do I put it?" I ask Mar-Beth later on the phone. "I have so much I want to give her and she leaves me with all of it."

"Alexandra, are you ready to leave her?"

"No," I answer.

"You still want her?"

"Yes," I answer.

"Then you will always be left with it. You will always be too much for her. She doesn't use you like you should be used. She doesn't call upon you, the full person, she only calls upon your understanding of her."

"But no one understands her like I do."

"Then that is your job in this relationship and you'll have to be satisfied with it."

Because my life must have her, I simply drive by and knock one day. Finally I meet the mother. She is large and murderous looking with iron-grey hair and wrinkles cut deep into her cheeks. When I arrive at the door she ushers me in. "Dorey is sleeping," she says. For a minute I am sure she will not have me in the house. "What happened?" she asks, she is standing by the porcelain sink looking almost ghostly. She is large and perfectly square in her housedress. Her grey hair is long, braided, and tied into a bun on top of her head. Her eyes are coal black like her daughter's. "She hasn't spoken to me since she came back from that trip. What happened up there?"

"I don't know," I say, shaking my head.

The mother takes her cigarettes from the table, taps one out, and pauses to light it on the stove. "It is her father's fault. He pampered her. He raised her to be king. He flies in from France once every five years to spoil her—to ruin everything I have tried to teach her. He tells her that she can do anything; that she is a great thinker. So she sits at home, doing nothing nearly all the day; she reads, she writes—but she never works. I tell her, 'Yes, you are a great little thinker—my little one—but the world will only remember you if you work and work hard!' She tells me I am being too European. That that is not the way Americans think. So, she thinks she can do anything, including carrying burning logs across the room. She thinks she's a little Jesus Christ that one! You go to her now, I've had enough of that one."

There is a dark oak door in the back of the house. I push the door open and see Dorey sitting cross-legged on the bed in the dark with her bandaged hands resting on her legs. She's staring at them. This image I love for some inane reason.

"What are you doing here?" she asks.

"What do you think I'm doing here?" I try to be cavalier and hate myself for it.

"I don't know, what are you doing here?"

"I met your mother."

"So now you know."

"Know what?"

Dorey is weary. She turns, she cradles herself toward the wall. "She's a drunk. She is the dragon lady."

From the kitchen I hear the mother shouting, "Well at least she is home now this one. We will see how long it lasts."

Dorey shouts for her mother to shut up.

"Sometimes she disappears for a month!" the mother yells from the kitchen.

"Shut up!"

"She never tells me where she goes!"

"Shut up!"

"Dorey," I say. "Shhhh." I am still standing by the door in the dark.

The door is open a crack. Dorey heaves herself out of bed, slams the door, shouting, "Shut up!" to the mother in the kitchen. The door will not latch closed. She slams it again and again and again.

"Don't bother," the mother says. "I am leaving."

"Dorey," I say. "Don't tell your mother to shut up."

She turns at me, vehement. "You shut up. You shut up if you want to stay here. I want everyone in this house to shut up and leave me alone!"

I hear the mother gather her keys and close the door behind her. Dorey stands at her bedroom window looking out. She is wearing an old blue robe; her hands hang limp at her sides. "She's gone," she whispers, then turns to me and says, "Are you only here to get a look?"

"Jesus, Dorey. No. I came to see how you were."

This seems to have some effect on her. She moves to the bed and pats the covers. "Come here," she says. "Lie by me. It's almost over. Tomorrow the bandages come off. I will return to classes. I will find a job, get an apartment. I can't stay here anymore."

"How have you been?"

"OK, why?"

"Have you been with Ann?" I ask. I figure she has been so I figure I would just ask.

"She may have come. But only to visit."

"What did you talk about?"

"Stop it. Stop all this obsessing. This talk of Ann is one more way you have of analyzing the whole relationship. One more way in which you try to determine if I love you. I do love you, damn it! That's it. I love you."

"You're asking me to trust you. I can't."

"Stop," she says and puts her hands on my shoulders. She asks me to light the candles and I do. She asks me to lie down and put my hands at my side which I do. She tells me that I have been shot by the enemy. I had been hiding out in a cave but they found me and shot me. And now I must take my clothes off so that she can take care of my wounds. I lean up far enough to slip off my pants and my blouse. "And now you must be still or they will find us." I am still as I watch her and her bandaged hands gently maneuver around me.

In the morning I hear her mother singing. I go out in the kitchen. There are plants, there is a bread warmer on a small counter by the stove. I had not noticed the night before how quaint the house was. There is, on the porcelain sink, an old cookie jar in the shape of a lamb. The mother's face is creased, well-lived, not as sinister looking as the day before. "You must help her, Alexandra," she says. "You are studying to become a teacher. You have patience that I maybe do not. I think she'll try to end her life."

I am smirking.

"Why are you laughing?" the mother asks.

"Because I think she is too egotistical to end her life."

"You don't think that suicide is egotistical?" the mother asks.

It stops me, this question. "Dorey is too scared to do it," I respond.

"Don't say that. If she hears you, she will do it just to spite you!"

"Well, anyway, she is not egotistical. She is stupid," the mother says, and holds her hands up in the air to indicate Dorey's hands. "But the very egotistical and the very stupid commit suicide."

From the bedroom I hear Dorey scream, "Mother stop! Stop talking to my friends about me!"

"And she is an impossible tyrant!" the mother says. "A little Napoleon!"

"How is she?" she whispers now so Dorey won't hear.

"Mother, shut up!" Dorey screams.

The mother leaves for work. She leaves me with a note for Dorey, some juice and muffins.

An hour later I give Dorey the note. Her hair is in her face. I brush it back.

"What does the note say?"

"It says she loves me."

She lays the note down and looks at me. "I wanted to hurt myself . . . before I hurt anyone else," she says. "That's why I did it."

We hold each other. She cries.

So Dorey calls a few days later. She is healed.
She is back at school. She has gotten a small job at
a marketing firm. Let's have dinner. I agree to dinner.

Later, I am playing with my spinach salad. We
are on our third glass of wine. Just our being together
makes me nervous for the first time. For this reason
I begin talking, a sort of nervous prattle, about my life
and how I don't know what the fuck I am doing
with it.

"That's because you have everything," she says.
"Every possibility is yours."

"Not true," I say.

"Really, you are too obsequious considering all
that you have. You have all the goods. Good family.
Good money situation. Good friends. Good house.
Good fellowship at the University. I don't know what
I can possibly be to you, or how I can possibly help
you."

"God, Dorey, don't say that. You're everything
to me."

"Only because you need a new project or something. Alexandra, take responsibility for your own
life, not mine. You can't save me, all right? I have to
save myself."

"Dorey, fuck it. Fuck all that shit! Let's do it!
Let's just do it. You asked me to stop all my intellec-
tualizing. And you have to stop, too. Can't we just live
together? Do we have to think about how I might be
saving you or you saving me? Can't we just do it?"

"I'm sorry." She shakes her head. "I'm sorry."

I take a deep breath. "Jesus, you take the wind
right out of my sails every single time. I mean, I
haven't even gotten to the part about how incapaci-
tated I feel in life. I haven't gotten to the part where

I tell you how it's getting god damned tiring, all this back and forth stuff. I haven't gotten to the part where I yell about how much remorse, frustration, impotence and ANGER I feel every day of my life thinking about this thing. How it is killing me. I haven't told you how it is killing me. God, I am on a roll. It is cathartic to finally get it out. I need to say it. 'You're killing this thing, you know. You are strangling the hell out of it with your inaction.' There, I have said it."

She says, "I'm sorry. I'm not ready."

"God, I have heard that a thousand times. WHEN will you be ready?"

She looks down at her hands. "I love you. Accept that for now. That's all I can say."

I take a breath. "I give up."

"Come on," she says. We go back to my house. We collapse in the bed.

In my bedroom we light candles. Dorey picks up a glass of water and dips her hand in it and then holds her hand above my eyes. Droplets fall from her fingertips. I try to catch them with my tongue. Later I begin to scratch at her arm. I find that if I scratch lightly, again and again, over the same spot, eventually it will bleed. Soon I create a long sore on her arm.

"Fascinating, isn't it?" I ask.

"Yes," she says, "because it seemed you were barely touching me."

She gets up and walks around, pouring the water on the candles. I take towels and drape them over the windows, so the morning light won't seep through the tiniest crack. We meet mid-house, in the dining room, beneath the chandelier. She takes my hand and places it on her breast. "Tell me true," she says, "how much do you love me?"

I stare out the window at the pink sky and begin: "I have loved you my whole life. And I love you with my whole life. When I was five you were my pretend playmate. When I was seven I was already in bed, dreaming of kissing you. When I was nine I saw you down the block playing ball with the boys and I thought of touching you. When I was twelve I sat in my room, listening to records, dreaming of dancing with you. I have been waiting for you my whole life. My whole life I have been waiting, don't you see? I was haunted as a little girl. I was haunted by you."

She is holding me, cradling me on the bare floor under the chandelier. She is crying. "I'm sorry if I've disappointed you," she says.

"You haven't disappointed me. You haven't," and I am cradling her, too.

She is crying harder. I tell her not to cry. "I'm sorry," she says. "I'm sorry that my desire to fuck up is stronger than my desire for you."

I rock her. "You're not fucking up. You're not."

She covers my face with her hands. She plants small kisses on my eyes. She is over me, like a wave from the ocean and I am swallowed. We both are indomitable in our moment. We fall asleep on the floor. When I awake again it is noon. I am filled with the purity of the feeling. I want to wake her and am afraid to.

In the following weeks we become a regular couple. We have dates and go to movies—and galleries where we run into the "art crowd." We go to parties and take walks and fall into bed at the end of it all.

We are at The Small Cafe again, Dorey and I. It is hot and hazy out. We sip Sangria. Dorey leans over to give me the edge of her glass. I drink from it. She wipes my lips. I mention sex. She smiles . . . embarrassed . . . we leave.

Another time we are in the bedroom. There are gauze sheets on the walls, a drawer full of scarves. She says, "A catastrophe could occur. It could happen at any moment. So do not look." The scarf comes floating down on my eyes. I am beyond love. I am in another world completely.

One morning she asks me, "Will you love me forever?"

"Forever," I respond. Then I am silent. I am silent because the word "forever" seems forced between us. It didn't sound like it was supposed to. And I couldn't say to her, "Dorey, when we say 'forever' it doesn't sound like it's supposed to." I am filled with dread at times that it is all acting.

I am visiting home. I walk in the door and my mother is there sitting in the kitchen. She is wearing the green robe. Her white-grey hair is shiny and wavy from a recent shower. I sit down to talk.

"What do you think of the latest launderette?" she says. Lately, my mother and father have made a small fortune by opening laundromats that have tea gardens, work-out rooms, and large-screen TVs over the dryers. They have three laundromats now. Except they don't call them laundromats; they're called "Launderettes." They've named them after their children. "Thomas's Launderette," "Stretch's Launderette," and the most recent addition is "Alexandra's."

"I drove by it. The sign looks bigger. Is it bigger than Thomas's or Stretch's?"

"A little. Redesigned, mainly," she says.

The launderettes seem to be their newest way of saying "I love you." It's hard to say "I love you," in my family. People start crying all over the place when you say "I love you." And so instead they give out money and open trust accounts for us with profits from the launderettes . . . etc. . . . .

"It's colorful. I like the pale peach for the washers, the pale blue on the dryers. And then the walls are pink again, aren't they?"

"Well, that is part of the look we try to give our launderettes."

"I like it," I say.

Then she asks, "Do you know anything about the new girlfriend your brother Thomas has?"

"She's just like all the others, isn't she? Blond? Buxom? Why don't you ask him about her?"

"Well, I don't know, Alexandra. The only way I can find out anything about Thomas or the women he dates is by talking to you or Stretch. You know he never speaks to us," she says. "Not really."

"Well, he doesn't speak to me much either.

Since birth I cannot remember a single conversation that lasted more than ten lines." It is more of a statement made out of curiosity than viciousness.

"Stop all this right now. I don't like you talking that way about your brother. And if you asked me," she continues, "everyone in this family is strange. Strange and alone and jealous of each other."

"Mother," I say just to end it. "I didn't say I didn't like Thomas."

"I thought you did. It sounded like you did. And Alexandra, *we* are a family. And if you had nowhere left to go on the face of this earth, you would still have your family. You remember that."

I go downstairs. I flick on the TV. I go to Stretch's old room. I look at the punch bowl. I go back upstairs. She is sitting, wiping something back and forth across the table in front of her. It is a button, one she has pulled off her robe. I sit down and she gazes at the button and presses it into her palm. She speaks calmly, "You are all my children. I loved you all so much. And I want you to love each other as well."

"Stop it, Mother. Why are you saying that. We do love each other."

She cries, "Sometimes I wonder. We are all loners, Alexandra. Your father is, and I am, and Thomas is, and you, too. We never say the things we need to say."

"Mother, we always say the things we need to say. It's just that you keep thinking there's more."

"That's not true, Alexandra. There's a lot left unsaid in this family."

I am silent. I know she is right.

"Maybe Stretch is a little different, isn't he?"

It has always been her illusion that Stretch has been the one to turn out "right" among us. Not as "gay" and "different" as her daughter; not as aloof as Thomas; not as shy as the man she married. It is almost as if this is a great hope of hers. That Stretch would bring our family into the mainstream . . . that he'd come home one day with the secret to American happiness. He'd come home one day with a pile of friends, a pile of children, a pile of cars, toys, dogs and cats to go along with it, and she'd love it. She'd start crying on the spot from happiness. "What kind of bullshit is that?" I ask myself.

"I don't know, Mother. You keep thinking that Stretch is going to do it for us. I keep thinking that we each need to do it for ourselves. Go find your own happiness, Mother. Don't wait for Stretch to bring it to you."

"I'm not waiting," she says. "You don't give me enough credit, Alexandra. I'm not waiting for him to bring me MY happiness; I'm waiting for him to bring me some of HIS happiness."

"Mother, do you hear what you're saying? That your happiness IS his happiness . . . But it's not MY happiness. I know that."

"Alexandra, I love you all the same."

"All right Mother, if you say so."

"Well, I guess I wouldn't be the one to say, now would I? I guess only time will tell. Yes, I hope as you grow older time will tell you a thing or two. I have heard the same complaints from your brothers. They think that you've been the one to get all the attention all these years. What with your therapy and your suicidal episodes."

"I was never suicidal."

"We didn't know that. You WERE depressed. You wouldn't talk to us for nearly three years—from the time you were twelve till the time you were fifteen. You worried your father and brothers and all of us . . . And I'll tell you something else! . . . I'm glad you're not having children. If I had it to do over again, maybe I wouldn't have had *any* children! So there, you think you know everything. You don't. Your father and I just want you to be happy. Your way."

"Then quit WORRYING about my being happy. Please. It drives me crazy the way you two worry about my happiness. I double-think everything I do, wondering if it will make you and Father happy or not."

I sit across from her and hold her hand. I am thinking of her image of her great and perfect family . . . And how, compared to her image, our family is tragic. Absolutely tragic.

She hugs me. The moment has been hard between us. It is over. I think we are both relieved. She tells me there is iced tea in the refrigerator. She brings out a new fur coat: "A Fendi," she explains. She speaks of buying a Jaguar, but first she would have to find a garage space because she isn't going to buy the car just so some hoodlums could steal it off the streets. And god knows, garages are hard to come by in Lincoln Park and so she probably won't get the Jaguar, unless, that is, she starts looking for a new home, which she just might do— a little bit north— along the lake, and *with* a garage. She tells me that she has taped an old Judy Garland special, that it's a classic and that I should go into the TV room to watch it. That is that. I take the iced tea; I go in to watch Judy Garland. All is forgotten; I'm sure that is the idea.

Later, I make some macaroni and cheese. She still stocks eight boxes of this. And I go downstairs again with my plate just to clear my head. *Western Union* is on the TV down there, starring Randolph Scott and Robert Young. The opening lines tell you it's the story of the brave young men who suffered through all kinds of extremes to lay the first transcontinental telegraph lines. I like it when you have to read the beginning of the movie. It always makes me feel comfortable—like you're being set up for a good story. I settle in to watch. In one scene Randolph Scott is lying in the dirt on the open range, with his hands tied up behind him. The bad guys have taken off, left him there to die, but the fire is still going. Randolph Scott scoots over to the fire, sets his wrists in the flames for the longest time, and burns those ropes right off.

I think of Dorey.

I remember . . . my third or fourth date with her when she asked me in and as we sat on the couch she handed me a piece of paper. It was damp and crumpled up—full of sweat from her palms. I opened it and saw five blue valiums there.

"Valium?" I asked, just to make the point that I knew.

"I'm on it already."

"Why did you take it?"

"I was nervous," she said.

"Nervous? About what?"

"You," she said.

"Me? Me!" I was incredulous. "You're kidding!"

"No. You make me nervous."

"You're kidding!"

"I'm insecure around you."

"You're joking!"

"I am always on the precipice with you, always between falling and not falling. I wanted to major in literature. I dropped out. Now I'm taking marketing. I thought it was better . . . more practical. But now, I meet you, and you did it. You did major in literature and you got that scholarship and everything. Everything's yours, Alexandra. The whole fucking world is yours. And you stay around me." She shook her head. "I can't be what you expect me to be."

"Jesus."

"So I took valium."

"Jesus, Dorey. You took valium because I majored in literature and you didn't? You know you can hold your own when we talk about books."

"Doesn't make any difference. You're teaching and I'm not."

Soon she had a hard time talking. She was slow between words. And we hugged. Her skin seemed thicker. On valium she was a hot animal on a languid day. I was in love at that moment. I mean if I had to pinpoint the moment it would be Dorey on valium.

"I feel somewhat perverse," I said.

"Why?"

"Because I like you on drugs."

"You'll like me even more in a minute." She went to the bathroom and she came back dripping wet with a towel around her. She had wet-backed her hair. The water dripped down her neck, behind her ears.

She offered me valium. I took one. She took one more.

I took one more. We breathed heavily from the valium. Her limbs were weighted and I lifted each slowly and then let it drop on the bed. She lifted me, I think, and turned me over. It was like being un-curled from a wave. She hovered over me. Stayed there for the longest time. I rolled back around and stared up at her. We stared at each other like this for millenniums. Looking. Just looking. Finally I reached up and scratched her cheek. She seemed not to feel it. I scratched again, leaving some red marks. She looked warm and feverish; she descended slowly on top of me, making love. I could hear my own breathing inside my head. Afterwards we just lay criss-crossed upon each other like animals.

A few weeks after this I called and there was a message on her machine: "I am in Wisconsin for the weekend. Please call back on Monday."

I left this message on her machine: "Dorey, you asshole, you fucking asshole. Who are you in Wis-consin with?"

As it turned out she was in Wisconsin with Ann. Thus began our first series of breaking up and coming together. We did this for a year, until the night in the Cadillac, which was the final break-up.

I sit here watching *Western Union* and I get this sick feeling—like the world is not well and maybe I would always be on the god damned roller coaster.

My daydreaming is ended as the door slams and Thomas comes in. I go upstairs to put my plate in the sink. He goes directly to the refrigerator and pulls out the left-over macaroni and cheese. He sits at the kitchen table, where I am sitting, and with his face tilted directly into the bowl he says to me, "So, what's new?" Before I can answer he says, "What you reading there?"

"*Town and Country.* Mom gets it."

"What for?" he asks.

"I don't know," I answer, even though I do. I excuse myself to go brush my teeth.

I hear my mother shuffle in from the TV room where she has been watching the Judy Garland special again. She pauses at the table to talk with Thomas. I am finished brushing my teeth and now study myself in the mirror, listening.

She asks him about a deal he's putting together for the development of a shopping mall. Then she asks about the plane. He stops eating. I can hear him put down his fork. He says, "What about the plane?"

"What do you mean what about the plane," she says. It's true; Thomas knows all about the plane. He missed the airport. He crashed the plane.

"Mother, I don't want to hear it again."

"Your father and I have a lot of money tied up in that airplane."

"I'll get the plane back. I'll have it repaired."

"That's not the idea, Thomas."

"Then what?" he says and I swear I can hear his hands fidgeting with the fork.

"We don't want you flying. It worries us. We want to sell your plane. What do you think? We'll give you the money to buy a boat, how's that?"

He is nonchalant. "You can take the plane. I'll get one on my own."

She is crying again. Actually, I don't know this for sure, but I can feel it sort of and Thomas is silent.

Soon Thomas is on his way out the door. And she says, "You know your father and I bought that plane."

"I'll have it towed back. I'll park it in the damned yard for you. You can drink coffee and look at your plane. And I'll buy my own plane next time, OK?"

"Thomas. Don't talk that way to me. I don't want it back. I was just wondering if you had taken the responsibility to get it back to Chicago."

"Mother, I'll have the plane towed back by Tuesday."

I can tell he has stepped back in again, probably afraid to leave without making everything OK. We all try to do that in our family. We try to make everything OK to a fault.

"I'm worried," she says.

"Don't be. I'll be fine. Really." And then he is gone.

I'm standing in the bathroom staring at myself in the mirror. When the door slams, the mirror rattles. "Everyone in this family has a secret wish to kill themselves." He didn't hear her say it. He was already out the door. But I sure heard her. She repeated it several times.

I go back downstairs and sit on the couch. *Western Union* is ending. *Family Classics* is coming on. I wonder if I should call her, if I should call my machine and see if there is a message from her. I do neither. I am filled with a weariness.

What is it Mar-Beth had said to me . . . "Soon you will get out of this weariness business." I think of this and then I think of Dorey pressing her breasts to mine as we stood naked in front of a mirror. Her face was buried in my neck. Her teeth were deeply imbedded into the soft skin of my shoulder. I was shivering with pain and pleasure, thinking, "She will not vanish, not ever vanish from the face of the earth. She is too mythical to ever die."

Weeks pass and I do not hear from Dorey. Summer is fully bloomed. Mar-Beth calls to say she has a new apartment. She has moved in with Bob at his place on Lake Shore Drive. "Is it OK?" she asks.

"Of course it's OK," I say. "Why are you asking me if it's OK?"

"I don't know. I know how you are with women and independence and all that . . . But things were moving along with Bob and we decided we would give it a try."

"I'm happy for you," I say.

"You are?"

"You're in a better place than I am right now."

"I am?"

"I'm certain of it."

Then Mar-Beth asks about her.

"Her? Oh, Dorey? Nothing has changed."

I tell Mar-Beth that I will be by soon to see her new apartment. After I hang up I start thinking about Dorey. It seems that all conversations with all people lead to thoughts of Dorey. I decide to write her:

"Dear Dorey,

Where are you? I want you here. The children next door are crouched, waiting for grasshoppers to spring out of the weeds, into the air. Do you think we could find an equally summer-like thing to do?

New Decision: I've decided to become religious in life; I mean doing good for the sake of good—to forget oneself by doing good. How does that sound?

My birth took place for you. I meant to tell you that. Dorey, we are in the same place psychically, I know it. Though please call me to verify. Just a joke (I think). Yours—Alexandra."

Dorey calls. She leaves a message on my answering machine: "Your letter was wonderful. I love you. When can we live together?"

I leave a message on her machine: "I love you, too. When can we see each other?"

I come home that evening and there is another message on my machine: "I love you. I want to see you now."

I call again. She is not at home. I leave another message: "Where are you? I want to see you."

She calls and leaves another message on my machine while I am out at the store. "Tonight, I'll come by. Call me if it's not OK."

I do not call to cancel, but she does. On my machine she states that she is feverish, that she is staying home, but not to try to call her, she is unplugging the phone, she needs her rest, etc. . . .

One day I sit in the sparsely furnished office of a therapist, with the damn sun coming through the old venetian blinds, and she is smoking up a storm and I have fifty minutes to tell her what I feel. So I tell her that I keep seeing these images of Dorey kneeling and naked in the cabin, staring at the burning log and then at her hands, burnt, and then of her, crying. And I keep thinking of that. Why do I keep thinking of that? I answer my own question. I answer that maybe that is me. Maybe I feel just as destroyed and lonely and scared as Dorey. I think Dorey comes from the same place I came from, somewhere underground, underwater.

"I know Dorey. We understand each other," I tell this therapist. "I know that she fears that she will never be loved, isn't worth being loved, and that sad reality compels her to harm herself, you see, and ideally, if she succeeds in destroying herself, physically, emotionally, whatever . . . then the prophecy has come true: she's not worth loving. I know that. No one else knows that. Only I know that. Me and one other person in the world knows that. Me and Dorey."

The therapist responds by saying, "Alexandra, anyone in the world would know that." She tells me to come back the next week. She ends with, "Why don't you concentrate on yourself this week. Next week come in here and tell me what you've learned about yourself!"

"I think this whole analysis is bullshit." This is what I tell her the moment I walk into her office the next week. "The whole world has got women believing they're crazy. There is nothing wrong with me; and nothing wrong with my falling in love with Dorey and wanting to check *out* of this existence. In this existence we are dying . . . everywhere . . . by bombs, by disease, by drugs, by murderous men . . . the bullshit in this world is killing me, like boys who bash fags, and men who beat and murder and rape their wives . . . and homophobic fascists who talk about god. . . . Where are all these people with fucked up heads? Why aren't they working on *their* shit?

"And another thing . . . Where's my story? Where's my story in history, in science, in literature? Where's my god damned story? Where's the lesbian women's story? Why should I want to be part of something that society conspires to keep me out of?

"I've had it. It's sick out there," I say.

"It can be sick in there too," she says and she points to her head, then indicates mine.

"I'd rather be sick in here than sick out there," I say.

So the second session ends with my anger at the world in general. The third session does not get much better as I am convinced that my life with Dorey is sweet compared to all the lies.

The therapist takes notes. Maybe she's thinking it is hopeless. It is. I don't need therapy. I need another world.

"Are you happy with Dorey?" she asks.

"No. I am ecstatic with Dorey."

"Ecstatic? That's a strange word to use."

"She is my drug."

"Why do you need a drug?"

"Why wouldn't anyone?"

"Lots of people don't, you know."

"They don't know any better. They think they're 'happy.'"

"You don't think there's such a thing as

happiness?"

"It's a ridiculous concept. They just killed two thousand people in Iran with germ warfare. My grandfather committed suicide. My aunt died of syphilis. Nobody told me. I had to guess. Big family secret, you see, it's all lies."

"Why should all that matter to you?"

"Why shouldn't it?"

"But what does it have to do with Dorey?"

"Dorey understands it."

I don't see how this therapist can disagree with me, but she does. I never return to see the therapist again. It is a waste of time since I know I do not want to belong to her world.

I go home. As I sit on the couch and think of the therapist, there is a rap at the kitchen window. It is Dorey, standing at the back window with wine, candles, and towels in her hands. "I've come to bathe you!" she yells. I go put on my robe. "Hurry up!" she yells. "It's freezing out here!" When I reach the kitchen I find she has drawn our names in the window with her finger. I let her in. She takes my hand and leads me immediately to the tub. She puts the water on, brings all the candles into the bathroom and lights them, pours the wine. After we have both taken baths, we wrap ourselves in towels, sit on the bathroom floor and talk half the night. Later, we move to the bedroom to make love. When we are through making love Dorey says, "You've touched me deeply. How many women in this world can do that for another woman?"

"Somehow, that's what I was trying to tell that therapist," I say.

Dorey arrives at my door again that week. She is crying. She is afraid her father is dying. "Why do you think he's dying?" I ask.

"Because he will. He will die before I get a chance to get to know him and tell him I love him."

"I thought you hated him."

She ignores this. "Why doesn't he come here?" she says.

"He's older," I say. Then I say, "Fuck that invitation shit. Just go. Show up on the bastard's doorstep. He'll love it. I guarantee it."

She cries. I hold her. We make love that afternoon. We make love long and hard. She cries when she orgasms.

For some reason I do not hear from her for two weeks and I am afraid to call her. I am afraid everything is wrong.

I call and leave a message on her machine. "I love you. I think of you all the time. I think that someday if I think of you hard enough I might be able to become you or become your child, your mother. I want to be. I want to be. I want to be . . . full of you." I say all this into the machine and realize immediately that it is a rather neurotic thing to do. I hang up; I call back. "I didn't mean to say all that. I just meant to say 'I love you.' " I hang up. And then I feel neurotic for calling back. "Fuck it. Just fuck it all," I think.

One day I am sitting across from her at The Small Cafe and not wanting to eat, just not wanting to eat. I am not interested in food. Eating makes me feel so nauseated— if I eat I will not be able to feel her, to touch her, if I eat, I will be lying. On the way home she takes my hand and says, "But Alexandra, you didn't eat and it made me so sad." And later when we are in the kitchen she puts a piece of bread in my hands and asks me to eat it, which I do, and she unbuttons my blouse and touches my breast as I eat the bread which is the beginning of our lovemaking.

Suddenly, she stops. "I'm afraid," she says.

"Of what? I love you."

"I'm afraid you're too much for me."

"Fuck that shit. I don't want to hear it, EVER!"

She walks out the door. Just like that. I am left holding the door and with it the enormous stillness of my apartment.

Later I call her. "Fuck you," I say to the machine that answers. "Fuck you. And I want to break up, too, if that's what you're thinking."

A month or two passes. Dorey and I have an agreement. The agreement is to stay the hell away from each other while we think things out. In the meantime I figure she'll get back together with Ann, which is what I hear she does. I go back to my therapist who now tells me that I am not so crazy, that life is worthwhile, that I just need to be alone. I agree with the therapist on the simple grounds that it wasn't working with Dorey, ever!

But Dorey calls me one day. She needs to talk.

She wants to be truthful. And my gut still tells me I love her, so I go.

So I go up Klyfield to Dorey's house and park in front of her mother's bungalow and I find Dorey out back with her legs strung on either side of the old lawn chair. She is under the tree and there is a decanter next to her. It has cognac. She gets up to greet me. She wears her dark sunglasses. They work. They work to intimidate me and make me think I don't know her. She smiles and pushes something into my hand. It is a chocolate kiss. "Eat it before it melts," she says.

She turns around, undisturbed, and goes back into the house. She comes out again carrying a white blanket. She spreads it out under the tree. We both sit there. The tree above is infected with worms. I can see the white husks of the worms speckled all over the leaves, causing the leaves to bend inward from the weight of these husks. My mind suddenly becomes plagued with doubt: "It won't work. It has never worked. You love her. It will work. What is love, anyway?"

After we are both situated on the blanket she asks how I feel. I seize the opportunity to respond.

"How do I feel? I feel angry. I feel you were never interested in this working. I feel you have fucked it up in every way possible, including your thing with Ann. I feel tired of all this back/forth shit. It's not going to work."

She is taken aback. "I want to work on it," she says.

"Are you going out with Ann?" I ask.

"What does that have to do with anything?"

"Look," I say, gaining speed, gathering momentum, anger . . . "I've been back and forth with you on this for years!! Years!! Fucking years!!! Now stop it! Stop pulling me along here. It's easy to resolve. You make a choice. That's what life is all about, making choices!"

I take her black and white cat who is lying in the grass and I stick him in my lap and begin petting him just to calm myself.

"I'm tired of it," I say. "You don't have to explain anything. I'm tired. I've had it. We've broken up. Did you know that? Just thought I'd make it official."

Her face is suddenly ashen and serious. "But I've broken up with Ann," she says. "I broke up with her last night. I want to go out with you."

"God, Dorey. Oh, god. This is it! This is funny! The classic case of being too late. This is it."

"Don't laugh."

"So now what?"

"What do you mean, 'Now what?' Now we can be. Just BE. Together!!!"

"And . . . what does that mean? Do we live together? Forever? Find an apartment? Pick out some furniture together? Take vacations to the Rockies. Have coffee together in the morning. Is that what it means?"

"Yes," she answers.

"I wanted to do that years ago. I don't want to do it now."

There is silence. "Why not?" she asks meekly.

I rub the old cat's belly. There are small tumors there. "Your cat has tumors," I say.

"I know," she says. "Leave my cat alone," and she yanks him away from me. She hugs the cat.

"Look, I'm glad you broke up with her," I say,

"but I just don't see how this is going to work now, because now I'm tired and I want a relationship that is easier, simple, kind . . . "

"God, I hate you," Dorey says.

"I want to stop," I say.

"I guess I want to stop, too," she says. "Because I'll be damned if I'm going to let you stop without me. You can't!" She begins to cry into her cat.

We pour more brandy. It happens suddenly, that she leans over and kisses me. The cat jumps out of her arms. Cars of summer whizz by on the street out front. The neighbor comes out to get something from the garage. The laundered sheets on the line next door swing in the breeze. Things move in a quiet way, and it seems to be like a vacuum after a bomb has hit, and the vacuum is drawing us together. And I know that I have ten more minutes, or perhaps half an hour, to make everything beautiful again.

Her body is dark and soft on the white blanket. I embrace her.

We sit on the blanket rocking each other.

"Dorey," I say. "We have to leave each other. We have to become more real in the world and the only thing we do together is hide. I have to become more of a person—the kind that has some good friends to talk to now and then. The kind that goes swimming and goes to movies. The kind that takes a French class and goes to political functions."

"It sounds pathetic," she says.

"It's not pathetic. It's life."

"You can't really LIVE that way and believe in it."

"I want to try."

"And I suppose you'll be joining a health club soon, and after that you may meet a man, that one who can understand women, truly, and after that you will be thoroughly brainwashed!"

"Jesus, Dorey, we have to stop this, you know?"

"I know," she says softly. "I'm afraid of your leaving me, though. I'm afraid of never seeing you again." She starts crying. Then I start crying. Stupidly, we kiss. She takes my hand and leads me into her bedroom. I'm thinking No, but I'm doing it. Yes, I am.

"We've got to stop doing this," I whisper as she holds me.

"We can't," she says.

So I guess I didn't stop it. I mean even though I wanted to I didn't.

I drive out to Wheaton to visit Diana, where she and her new girlfriend, Ellen, are living just a few blocks from Diana's mother. Ellen is at school. So Diana and I sort of hang out in a way that is reminiscent of high school for me. We go to the White Hen and buy mango popsicles. We play catch with an old ball and mitt. My hands become sticky inside it from the popsicles. I am feeling small and nostalgic for childhood. We stop playing ball and she asks me to come stand next to her.

"I have an art scholarship," she says, brushing herself off. "I wanted to tell you. I will attend the Sorbonne next year."

"Great, that's great. Congratulations!" I say. But for some reason I feel weird about it. I had always thought that Diana would be there for me. Maybe I had harbored this thought that when it was finally over with Dorey, I would have Diana. I don't know. Way back there. I mean WAY back there, maybe I thought I'd be with Diana someday. When all the craziness was over with Dorey, I just sort of thought Diana would be there, in some preserved state or something, waiting for me. "And Ellen?" I ask.

"She'll join me in a couple of months. She's a computer programmer. And she speaks French. She's applying for work permits. We'll get an apartment together."

"Great," I say. "I'm happy for you." I sit on the couch in the garage and I realize I feel sick. Diana kicks off her shoes and brings a photo album of her and Ellen over to me.

"I am very happy for you," I say.

The sun is setting behind the houses across the street. I smell supper in the suburbs. Beef. The mitts are at our feet. Her hair is all over in her face. When we are done with the photo album I say it: "I will miss you."

"And I will miss you," she says. At that moment we both know that nothing will ever come of it. It scares the hell out of me.

Later, when I am in my car, she leans in and kisses me good-night. A soft, friendly kiss. It nearly kills me.

Later, Mar-Beth says to me. "You're just growing up. You can't have everything you want. Some things you have no control over."

But still I go back to my apartment and I dream. I dream of slow women carrying buckets of water on their heads. I dream that I stand naked in their rivers while they pour the water over me. When I awake I masturbate, I watch the sunset, I go back to sleep.

Weeks later I call Diana in Paris and it is a strange overseas call. We don't know what to say. "I love you," would be too much . . . not enough . . . ridiculous. I ask her what she has been doing. She and Ellen have found bookshops and cafes. They have made new friends. They shop at the market and have hired a French tutor. "And Dorey?" she asks.

"I don't know," I respond. "I haven't spoken to Dorey lately."

"Maybe you are finally over it," she says. "I'm happy for you." And I get this sick feeling later on, that Diana is way past me, and leaving me further behind.

And then it is late summer. I am cleaning the house one day when Dorey calls. She wants to know if I have thought about it . . . if we can try again.

So Dorey comes by. We have a "date," as arranged. It is night. Warm. The windows are open. The cat is on the rug. I've rented two videos. I make popcorn and a pitcher of lemonade. I want it to be regular. Please, let us be regular. I nearly suggest that we go grocery shopping together. But then we sit on the couch and touch, gently. Dorey is wearing a whitc T-shirt. She has perspired around her neck and so the T-shirt sticks to her skin there and of course, I look at it.

I sit in the chair opposite, but lean forward far enough to play with the neckband of her T-shirt, and then I run my fingers under the sleeves of her shirt, nearly reaching down to her breast. And then I start scratching her arm, lightly. She has thick skin. I mean I could never see her veins, just smooth, thick skin. So I scratch and scratch at the thick coat of skin on her arm, wanting to what? Mar her? Somehow peel back her skin—get underneath her? Leave a mark on her too-perfect creamy physique? Already it is not regular. The popcorn sits in the metal bowl in the middle of the table. It is never eaten. The movies are never taken out of the plastic bag they came in. She never drinks the lemonade. I just keep scratching over the same spot. Blood finally appears. First small dots of blood appear, then the mark becomes deep red and filled-in and we just stare at it.

Then the two of us rise as if cued and walk to the back porch. We hear the neighborhood horn player; he is playing near a window somewhere. She stands at the porch railing. I go in for a moment to get the vodka out of the freezer. The bottle perspires in my hands as I pour. We drink vodka on the porch. My petunias in the pot at our feet are consumed by spider mites. I make note of this. I mention it to Dorey. She looks at the plant disinterestedly. We stare out at the porches across from us as we listen to the horn player. Sometimes her hand touches my back and I feel something wrong. I feel her trying to reassure me with her touch at my back. Why? Of what?

I wish the flowers were prettier and that everything in the house were perfect. That the comedy was in the VCR, that we were laughing. But we are standing at the porch rail overlooking the garden. Virulent summer rains have turned everything verdant. You can't make out the ferns from the weeds, the trees from the vines. We stand. A car snakes by in the alley. A white car. It is slow. It seems we have summoned it. I feel the slowness. Dorey and I turn to each other as the car passes.

And I'm thinking, "This is NOT a date. I know this. I don't know what the hell it is. But it's not a date. How the hell is it that Dorey and I relate to each other?" I am vaguely aware of telling myself that I am not doing what Diana and Ellen are doing at this moment. Then I am vaguely aware of telling myself it is something more. Dorey and I are more.

We walk inside. I, following her. We sit in the kitchen and have more vodka. In the living room we finally put the movie in, with the volume off. We put an old Marvin Gaye album on the stereo. We have our vodkas in front of us. We sit on the couch, stare at the TV. Dorey takes the cat in her lap and nips at his nose with her lips. I play with the shoelaces of her one foot which is crossed my way. Soon we lie one upon the other on the couch. We brush each other's hair aside, and brush and brush. Her hair keeps falling back in her eye. I keep brushing it aside. She looks at her sore and the scab that is forming. Hypnotic. It is time for bed. Candles. I hang towels from the window so that the light won't enter in the morning. She has a cold, a fever, a stomach ache, she tells me. I give her Tylenol. Aspirin. Nyquil. I find some old codeines in the bathroom. Then she sits up in bed and feeds the same to me. We are drugged now. The both of us. We fall asleep.

I wake up in the middle of the night, in a sweat, needing to talk with her. She lies complacent, luminescent, dead asleep. So I sling my arm over her back and curl near her side and fall asleep.

We awake the next morning. The sun comes in through a gap in the towels, falling in a two-inch stream across the bed. Dorey bolts up when this wedge of sun hits her eye. She looks at me, then slides back in bed. Three hours later she wakes up again. I am reading in the living room. I think there is an understanding between us that she will leave quietly and that I will allow her to do so. She stands in the living room to say good-bye. She says she'll call. She slips out the door.

She does call and she gets my answering machine. I am beginning to think that she only calls when she knows the damn machine is on. Anyway, she is ill, and she doesn't see getting together in the near future.

I figured I'd get a call like this because I am feeling the strangeness between us, too.

Then Mar-Beth calls to tell me she loves the apartment on Lake Shore Drive which she shares with Bob, but she's not so sure about Bob any more . . . Anyway, there is a rooftop pool and a rooftop patio around it . . . Bob is working tonight and do I want to come over . . . "We'll have drinks at the pool, that sort of thing."

You can see clear to downtown. It is the kind of view that makes you believe in fairy tales. On one side is the lake and the stars and standing flush against this sky are the giant skyscrapers. Far off in the distance below us we can see the line of ant-cars snaking around the skyscrapers and continuing down Lake Shore Drive.

And there Mar-Beth is, behind me, sort of ushering me over to two redwood reclining chairs. She has her straw hat on, her white robe and green two-piece, she carries a pitcher of martinis, two glasses, her cigarettes and lighter. Static heat-lightning flashes across the dark sky. The pool is that calm, turquoise blue, coolly ready for a love scene.

So I set down my glass for a refill and Mar-Beth sets down her martini and says, "The clouds are rolling in. It gives you goosebumps, doesn't it?"

Nostalgically I say, "Yeah, Mar-Beth. For some reason I'm thinking of being a kid at camp, under the tent when it rains."

And I think that this is a grand moment to go down in the annals of grand moments on rooftop pools twenty-four stories up with a view of downtown Chicago and with a storm coming in over Lake Michigan. I am still clocking things—like life—I am still clocking life, saying all the time, "Now that's a grand moment, a perfect moment. Now, I feel alive. Thank god I feel alive, finally, I *feel* without question, I *feel*." And I don't know why I can't get beyond these moments, but I can't.

So it is lightning and the pool is cool and gleaming in front of us. Spotlights shine up from the bottom. Mar-Beth smokes slowly, like Hedy Lamarr.

She gazes at the sky and I gaze at the light refracted on the blue surface of the pool. Mar-Beth says, "How often does one get a thunderous sky and a cool blue pool in one glance?" There is a half-moon near the Sears Tower. "It looks like someone had stretched their arm outside the window of the 75th floor and put the moon there, stuck it there with some school glue," says Mar-Beth. I nod in silent agreement.

Mar-Beth sips her martini. "I don't think it will work out between Bob and me," she says.

"Oh shit, Mar-Beth."

"What?"

"Well, just shit. I wanted something to work out for someone in this world. I wanted to hear about love."

"Sorry. He's too critical. First, he doesn't like the idea of my working as a waitress to support my acting career, then he says I'll never make it as an actress because I don't have enough confidence in myself, and I'm thinking that maybe the reason I don't have enough confidence in myself is because I keep going out with men like him!"

"Well, then give it more time." I am trying to be supportive.

Mar-Beth shakes her head. She sounds old/wise. She says, "No, I know what kind of man I want."

The electrical storm over Lake Michigan is brewing. Five shots of electricity, looking like fingers ready to strangle, come toward us out of the dark. The pool flashes yellow, then black, then yellow. Mar-Beth says, "How's Dorey?"

"It's gnashed. It's gone. It's dead."

"That's too bad. She was strange—a skittish

animal, but I liked her. That's not going to work either, huh?"

"No."

"Well, that's really too bad."

"Come on, Mar-Beth. I will allow you your break-up with Bob, if you allow me mine with Dorey."

"Dorey had a subtlety. Bob says she's probably the real thing."

"What does that mean?"

"Bob once told me that there are a few noble savages left on earth. He thought Dorey was one of them."

"She was."

"Thing is . . . animal passion is a cruel thing. It puts desire before love, and all that . . . bestiality isn't worth the cruelty that comes with it . . . that's what I've found. Anyway . . . " she grows silent.

"No, you're right . . . " I say faintly.

We drink lanquidly. We are quiet as we watch the electricity snake through the sky. "There's a bite mark on your arm," Mar-Beth says, leaning over from her chaise lounge to mine, to touch the scar. Indeed there are two half-moon shaped teeth marks there. They have been there for weeks. "Dorey did it," I respond. "I don't know, we were making love and she just bit me. Crazy, isn't it?" Mar-Beth smiles slyly. I smile. For a split second we know. We know and we will know it a thousand years back and a thousand years coming. We are animals.

I decide to jump in the pool. An electrically charged shot of thunder nearly touches down to the waist-level water I am standing in. Mar-Beth jumps back and insists that we leave and retreat to her apartment downstairs.

"Fuck," I say, getting out of the pool. "Fuck, I was hoping it would nail me."

Today in the supermarket they ask me what I want and I do not know the answer. I don't know why the clerk should notice me in the aisle and come up to me to ask me what I want. There are thirty others with baskets. Why not ask one of them? Then, it may have looked like I was wandering. Or perhaps I looked like a thief, who knows. All I know is that I am singled out. That others must know about me, my insecurity, my lack of concentration . . .

So I go to my mother's house to visit, because I am thinking of Dorey again and would do anything for her at this moment.

I feel raw in the world. I sit across from my mother. She is reading her *Town and Country* and speaks to me over glances from the page. "There was this woman in Saks today who looked like Marilyn Monroe. Where do all these women come from who look like Marilyn Monroe? What are they thinking of? I mean what's going on in those heads of theirs?" she says.

I laugh. What a relief to laugh!

"Really, what do these women think who believe they look like Marilyn Monroe? Do they think they ARE Marilyn Monroe?" she asks.

"I don't know, Mother," I say, shaking my head.

"Well, I think they should wake up and smell the

coffee. I just want to shake each and every one of them and say, 'wake up, wake up!' "

"Why don't you?" I ask.

"I've got enough with my own family," she says and for some reason this hits me as true.

"Besides," she says more reflectively, "some people are dreamers, and can only function as dreamers, and maybe the dreamer is of some value to society. Maybe they are supposed to be that way, naturally." Then after pausing she adds, "I don't have the luxury to daydream. I wish I did."

"I'm a dreamer," I say.

"You don't have to tell me, Alexandra."

"I like to dream."

"I worry about you," she says. "Your father worries, too."

Later, I go downstairs and turn on the TV with the volume down. I sit in the dark. I am thinking of Dorey. I realize then, at that moment, that I have stopped longing for her. I have stopped, at least, my idea that we should be married. And then I realize that my not longing for her is the same as longing. I am still thinking of her. Only now I am thinking of *not* thinking of her. Very clever. Maybe someday I will think of how to not NOT think of her.

So I decide to spend the weekend at my parents' house. It is comforting to be there. It is summer and it is cool in the basement where I stay in the old guest bed. I spend my time remembering her.

I remember . . . the first time I fell in love with Dorey was probably when I was nine and fell in love with a woman named Barbara. If that makes sense . . . that one woman incarnates the other . . . Barbara lived in a yellow house two doors down. In the mornings she went to beauty-culture school. She drove a yellow Plymouth Duster. Her practice wigs would hang from her hands. I would kneel at the couch in the front window and watch Barbara go to her car, the lemon-yellow Duster. She had thin arms. She had a way of struggling with the car door, her wigs and her packages, which made her attractive. At night time she would go to the neighbor's stoop down the way. Boys would hang from the railings and tease her. She was shy. Always this image I have of Barbara, slightly tan, still sticky from her nightly ice cream cone, in a white knit blouse, saying, "Go on. Go on now," to the boys. And boys backing away, backing away toward the curb and running home screaming and racing with each other.

I write notes to Dorey that I will never send:
"I finally understand anger/hate/war. War is the only thing left that brings us to dying at a frontier. It used to be you could die crossing the ocean, crossing the plains, crossing a river. War is the only thing. And love."
I write to Dorey:
"Did I ever tell you about the worm? My worm? The one that's eating at my brain? Well, it's still there. I sit at my brother's old desk in the basement and I feel it crawling around in my brain. Becoming

friendly. I have visions of being old and having known you fifty years ago or something . . . and having it over, long over, but then suddenly I will be very old and walking down the street and I will catch a glimpse of myself, a reflection of myself in a shop window . . . and I will know that I am still waiting for you. Even when I'm eighty. The worm-thing brings me all these revelations. The worm-thing tells me that everything is beyond me."

So a few weeks later I am home and I call Mar-Beth and we go to the Indian Restaurant, our favorite place, the only restaurant in Chicago that fronts an alley. There is no one in the huge red dining room and I imagine that there is a war on and all the people in the city are at the front, fighting, but Mar-Beth and I have come to dinner. The waiter is handsome and clad in a white jacket. He wheels the food out on a little tray. Mar-Beth has asked him if he could leave the "yellow" off the rice. He serves us the clean, white rice and disappears. Mar-Beth tells me that an apartment with a little stand-up swimming pool is up for rent. "Can you believe it? Three bedrooms and a pool in the backyard. And right in the middle of the city! The elevated passes right overhead. It's incredible! You've got to see it and say you'll move in with me."

"And Bob?" I ask.

"Gone," she says. "And now we've got to take it. It may never come up for rent again. So how 'bout it?"

"Maybe," I say. "Let me think about it."

"Oh, don't be such a dolt!" she says and I like her

97

for saying this. "It is only a small above-ground pool, but to find it in the middle of the city makes it a gem." I agree to move in. We drink wine to it. We get drunk. The waiter reappears after the curry dinner and Mar-Beth asks him if he might possibly have sorbet? No sorbet. Then peach sherbet perhaps? No sherbet at all. We laugh in our drunkenness—not at the waiter but at our idiotic questioning of him.

I spend the next month busying myself, preparing to move in with Mar-Beth. I decide during this time to buy new things for my new house. I take up tennis again, become a Girl Scout leader, volunteer for the Red Cross. I get all kinds of ideas. And still sometimes it feels like so much invention; it feels as if I have contrived a life just so that I can forget her.

I busy myself—intensely busy myself, moving in with Mar-Beth. It is a three-bedroom. I make one room the library. I am reading Blake. I am attracted to this proverb from Blake: "The prolific would cease to be prolific unless the Devourer as a sea received the excess of his delights."

I busy myself by writing notes to myself on little stick-'em pads, and then stick them on the refrigerator. I write: "Of this love for Dorey . . . I feel sometimes it is a perverse game I play with myself with a character like Dorey, but NOT Dorey. I have invented this character to rob myself of the consciousness that I don't want."

Then all life and life's "busy" efforts are reversed. She calls. She says she has been thinking of us, of the dream we had of being together.

I don't know anymore what the dream was. I want to say, "Dorey, what dream? Which dream do we speak of? The now dream? The later on dream? The dream. What dream? What is it again we were dreaming of? What a heap of shit this has turned out to be. What a heap of shit."

But we arrange a meeting. We go to our "Small Cafe" on Wabash. We drink like horses. She has a ring on which I do not recognize. She takes the ring off. "You put it on," she says, handing it to me, curling my palm around it. "I brought it for you."

It is a lie. I want to say: You are lying to me. Ann or someone else bought it for you. But hell, what is the difference any more?

She places the ring on my finger. "It's my ring to give," she says. I am sure it isn't hers to give. We drink more. I look at the ring. She caresses it. "What are we?" I ask. "What are we to each other?"

And we drink more. She takes the scarf off her neck and ties it around mine. We are quiet. My mind is drowned. I have forgotten everything. I want to go home but instead we go to a bar. This one is infamous for its drunkards. She takes me into the bathroom and caresses me and tells me that she loves me, she loves me, yes, she does. We exchange mad kisses in the bathroom. Back out in the bar we drink more. She gathers the bowls of pretzels, chips, popcorn, and we feed each other.

We fall out of the bar into the bright late afternoon sun. "We are in Oaxaca, in Madrid, we are in a sun-drenched parched land," I say. I put on my sunglasses and stumble. "And when we get home we're going to make mad, fucking love."

She takes me home. Mar-Beth is out. "Probably out with Bob," I slur to Dorey. Dorey rolls me into bed, covers me. She leaves.

Later I call her. "What happened?" I say.

"You were drunk," she says.

Silence. "I know I was drunk. I know THAT! But we didn't make love. We were going to make love, weren't we?"

"It didn't work out," she says.

"It never works out," I say.

For some reason she hangs up on me.

I pick up the newspaper one morning and read a story about an auto accident. In the car there was a child, a man and a dog. The car careened into the mountainside. The man, the child and the dog were each killed on impact and left scattered across the side of the mountain as points on a triangle, equidistant from the other. I wonder at the mathematical formula that might be involved in this. I wonder why it is so hard for me to distance myself from Dorey when a reactive energy should be equal to an active energy. Quite naturally and scientifically my distance from Dorey should be equal to Dorey's distance from me. I begin to wonder if the natural laws of physics won't bring me safety and comfort.

She calls and says she is coming over. I tell her not to. It is only from a great distance that we can see each other sharply and acutely, and only from this distance that we desire each other. As soon as we approach it all becomes flat.

I dream that she has come back to see me: She leans against the back door, holding it open, feet apart. The sun is white and the trees of the yard are stirring behind her. A violent wind comes, stripping branches of leaves. And then a shot of unbelievably warm air rushes in the kitchen and along with this some leaves get blown in and are swirling around her feet and blow right across the kitchen floor in front of me.

"Why?" I say. I draw it out. "Why are you here?"

She hugs me. There are eight other women in my kitchen, sitting on couches, and they all begin to clap. And I know that this moment is for the women and we are together for the women, but when we are alone we will not be OK.

I awaken. I call the therapist.

"I still want her and it's not working."

"Maybe it's not supposed to work," she says.

"I don't care. I don't care what you or anyone else in the fucked-up world thinks. Well, I'm throwing it away. I'm telling everyone to go to hell. I love Dorey and I love her because she is a dreamer and I don't care if she's the worst fucking person in the world for me, I need that. I need the dream."

"It will be you and Dorey and no one else," she says.

I see Dorey walking down the street a week later. She is dressed in black pants with a small black frock-type jacket. The frock moves loosely back and forth as she walks and she is peeling an orange. It is cool out. She has her black, calf-high boots on. I don't call to her. I follow her with my eyes. The boots disappear into the crowd.

My mother calls to tell me that I haven't called her. "What's up with you?" she says. "Why such a stranger?"

"I'm OK," I answer. And then there is silence because neither one of us wants to bridge the gap left by years of non-information. She begins:

"The Armstrongs invited your father and me out to their house last Saturday. They have a dog who should be murdered. The thing has torn up Libby's curtains. Shredded them. And Libby took down the curtains, threw them out, and the dog dragged them out of the garbage. She finally gave up and now the thing, the dog, sleeps on his pile of curtains in one of the bedrooms. Her new curtains are now HIS bed. Imagine, a dog, ruling the house like that! I would never allow it. I would have given that dog away to the first kid who passed on the street. Would you allow that? If it were my dog he'd be out on the streets."

"Mother, he wouldn't."

"Don't you believe it!"

"Remember when Serita chewed up your fur hat?"

"Oh, my fur hat," she says, nearly crying, remembering the incident. "My brand new hat. I nearly killed that dog. Didn't I?"

"I think you beat her with a gym shoe."

"Well, your father stopped me from killing her."

"That's funny, Mother."

"Why?"

"Because I don't remember Father stopping you. You're all bluff and so is Father."

"And so are you," she says.

"What, what do you mean?"

"Why such a stranger? Don't you want to come and see us?"

"I do. I will. I love you. I love you both, you know that."

"I'm not so sure we know that," she says.

"Mother, please. It's hard enough to say it, don't make me sky write it for god's sake."

And then she asks me if I would like to go to Italy and I am stunned. "Italy?" I ask.

"In the fall," she says. "Libby is thinking of meeting us there, that is, if you want to go."

"And Father?"

"You and I know very well that he'd rather go off with his men friends, and sometimes I'd rather go off with the ladies. It's what keeps us sane sometimes."

I tell her I will think about it. "And how is Dorey?" she asks.

"Dorey?" I say.

"Didn't you tell me you were going out with

someone named Dorey?" It kills me that she's finally now coming round to asking.

"Dorey's fine," I say.

"Oh, so everything's fine?" she says.

"I guess."

"What do you mean, 'you guess?' "

"We've broken up."

"Well, who's breaking up with whom?" she asks.

"Mother, what difference does it make?"

"It makes a difference. Look at what happened to Thomas. He was in a depression for eight months for a marriage that lasted eight months and if he would have beat her to the punch he wouldn't have been so depressed."

"God, Mother . . . "

"Mother, what?"

"Well, it's just that you have such a calculating way of looking at things."

"Now that I'm older I can be calculating. I'm getting your father a cane for his birthday. Did I tell you?"

I laugh.

"Do you think he'll like it?"

"I don't know. I guess. Yeah."

"So did you break up with this girl?"

I put my hand to my head, begin pacing across the apartment and in the process almost drop the receiver. "I guess we broke up with each other. It is mutual."

"Well, you take care of yourself," she says. "You and your brothers have a tendency to put your heads on the slaughtering block."

"What do you mean?"

"I mean don't over attach yourself. There are

other people out there for you. If this girl doesn't want you, don't you go chasing after her. Have more pride than that."

"I will, Mother," I say.

"And think about Italy. Fall is the right season for it. I should make airline reservations as soon as possible."

"All right, I'll think about it."

And then we hang up and I sit down and my thoughts are filled with her and what I think is that my mother has come a long way–that she is still hard, I mean a hard woman, hard to get to know but she tries, in her contained, deliberate way, to say I love you. And so I think of this. I think of this for a long time.

Dorey calls. I am in bed at at two a.m. when I hear the phone machine click on and her voice on the other end. She is drunk. She is at a men's bar on Ohio Street. She leaves the number. I crawl out of bed as I am compelled to do, and call her. And as the phone rings I wrap the covers back around me and sit in the bed waiting for someone at the men's bar to answer. It is quiet when the bartender answers. I ask for Dorey and he seems to know who she is.

"Dorey here," she says.

"What are you doing?" I ask.

"I'm drunk," she says and I can tell from the slur that she is. "I'm drrrrunk, why aren't you?"

"Jesus, Dorey, where are you? Why are you calling me now?"

"No one else ta call," she says. "No one else sees

me as the grrrreat person that you see me. Besides, no one else would understand."

"Understand what?"

"I'm dead. It's only a myth that I'm alive. You keep that going. Really, really, really, I'm dead."

"You're drunk. I'll call you another time."

"Don't you dare hang up on me. If you do, I'll beat you to the draw. I'll hang up first!"

"Hang up," I say.

There is a click. God damn if she hasn't hung up. As soon as I put the phone in its cradle, it rings again.

"The bartenders here are very nice," she says. "They keep dialing your number for me."

"Where are you?"

"Oh, it's great. It's just great here. I'm sittin' right at this here ol' bar, with the phone on the counter like I own the place and I have a bartender here who's memorized your number and I have a vodka on rocks in front of me and you here on the phone-thing and what more could a girl ask for in life?"

I am silent.

"You're silent, but you're critiquing me right now. I can tell. Your little head is going, 'Buzz, buzz, buzz. She's drunk,' you're thinking, 'plus she says she's dead. Did I really go out with this woman? Did I really?' you're thinking. 'How could I have?' "

"Dorey." I am particularly hit by her drunken honesty. "I'm not thinking that. I've given up on this, as I should have a long time ago, because we're different."

"Don't sssssay that. I want you now. I do. I really do. I didn't say it before, but I'm saying it now. I want you. I called because I've been thinking we shouldn't be so arbitrary about this thing. We've been too ARBITRARY. TOO ARBITRARY . . . like thinking maybe this will happen between us or maybe it won't. We should decide. Just decide. I want it, don't you? Let's decide now."

"Jesus, Dorey. Jesus. Now you want it. I knew this would happen. This is a fucking comedy, you know that? 'Cause now I DON'T want it. I DON'T want it. Things are never right between us. We're not like a regular couple and I don't think we could make it regular at this point."

"Regular! You want to be like THEM? All the liars out there? You fink. You traitor! You've turned over to the other side! You've been brainwashed by your god damned therapist! I knew it!" I hear ice cubes clink into the phone receiver and she pauses to order another drink from the bartender. "You stinking, rotten low-down scum! You traitor! Neither one of us watches TV, or has a Walkman. Neither one of us cares about the war in Central America or who's god damned president of the United States! Next thing you'll tell me you want to visit Walt Disney World—to become part of that whole passive pop culture out there. Well, they FIRE homosexuals at Walt's World! So there! There's America for you. And we're not regular. So there! Traitor!"

I jump on the opportunity to answer her charge. "Dorey, I don't want to be regular like them. First of all they're not all 'regular.' By regular I mean healthy and health is a relative term."

"Alexandra, I'm drunk. SSSpeak to me in English."

"Dorey," I say patiently, "I mean I want to be more REGULAR! I don't know how else to say it.

Boring. I want to be more boring, less dramatic. Your calling me drunk, like this, is dramatic. Instead of having THIS conversation, you should ask me what I did today. We never talk about what we did today. Every conversation is a now or never conversation."

"I'm sorry." She is crying. "I'm sorry I'm drunk right now, but I happened to be drunk and then I happened to want to call you. But don't say regular to me. It makes me cry. I don't know how to be regular. I hate that word. I hate that word now. I'm NOT regular. I'm alienated. I'm angry. I'm misunderstood . . . Alexandra, I need you."

"Dorey . . . I'm not sure . . . "

"Just a secon', just a secon'. I'm not finished here. Let me finish. Just let me finish. That's another problem, you never let me finish. You always have to get in the last word."

"OK, OK . . . " I say, to calm her.

"I'm lost. I can tell you that and you should believe me. I'm anxious all the time. I don't know what to do with myself and then I end up doing nothing. Maybe you're right. I'm not any good to you right now. I'm just a shadow-thing. That's what I am, a shadow-thing."

"Dorey, you're not a shadow-thing. You're anything but a shadow-thing. You're very real."

"Don't say that, you'll make me cry," she says.

She is quiet while she sips on her drink. "I miss your sex," she says suddenly.

"I miss your sex, too," I say because, truthfully, I do. I miss all of Dorey. "I miss all of you," I say.

"Our sex, our sex," she repeats. "It makes my mouth dry and nervous to think about our sex. Our sex. It is beautiful, Alexandra. I will never forget our sex."

"Why couldn't we get beyond it?" I ask. It is nearly a rhetorical question. It goes right past her.

"It was beautiful because it had a life of its own," she says.

"It couldn't make EVERYTHING OK," I say.

"No one else will ever be able to touch it," she says. "No one else in your life will ever be able to do what I did for you."

"Dorey," I say.

"Alexandra, it's true."

"I wanted it to work, badly. Yes. I did. Yes. I wanted it to work. I love you," I say. It is not something I meant to say; it is simply something I say. "But it can't work," I say to catch myself.

"But I have jus' one more thing to say," she continues. "Maybe I have a few more things to say. God, Alexandra. There was something wonderful there, wasn't there? I mean, I thought there was a lot of passion between us. And I don't see how it could have been wrong to be that passionate. I don't see how we could write it off as a mistake. Passion has purpose in life. It makes one feel alive. Most alive."

"Maybe not most alive," I say. "Maybe just most involved at that moment."

"You've been seeing too much of your therapist," she says. "We would have been . . . we would be . . . we would be immortal. Is that so bad? To look for immortality in love? To believe it is there? I felt it, didn't you? For a while? Didn't you feel there was no one else like us? No one else who would understand us? EVER?"

"Yes, I felt that way," I say quietly.

"And now you don't feel that way?"

"No."

"Why not?"

"I don't know. I found out that I have to understand myself, and my fears, before I can go to you, otherwise I'll always be looking for my definition in you."

"Jesus, Alexandra, what are you talking about?"

"I don't know," I say, because in a way, I don't.

"Jesus, this is civilized," she says. "I want to talk about sex again. SEX IS the book of revelations. The Bible of the subconscious. The flames that melt ice. The light in the darkness. The poetic genius, a mean genius—that was our SEX. And you're still thinking about it, aren't you?"

"Dorey, stop it. You know better."

"Look," she says. "Look, I'm sobering up here and I don't want to have to get drunk all over again. I'm drunk and I needed to get drunk just to say this. So let me say it 'cause I don't wanna have to get drunk again."

"OK."

"I want to say . . . I want to say . . . that it lasts. It lasts. It lasts. It lasts in the sky, in the universe, it lasts. Our passion is out there. It's floating around in the sky, or putting raindrops on earth, or putting the heart in the next baby. Our sex is out there."

I am silent for a moment because I like to think of it that way, too, sometimes, but then I say, "It wasn't enough."

"All right," she says. Then, "Shhhh. Shhhh. Please. You're bringing me down."

"How is Ann?" I ask. This statement comes suddenly, out of the blue. But I have a need to put everything in perspective. To say, look, there have been other women, there will be other women. Life goes on.

"She's good," Dorey says. "Actually maybe I will see her again. Maybe not. I have to think about it. Anyway! She is much less demanding of me than you are. No talks about life or death or god or sex and religion or anything like that, thank god."

"Thank god," I say.

"I miss you," says Dorey. She is crying. "I'll miss you. I miss you now," she says. "Badly."

"I miss you too, baby."

"I really miss you," she says.

"And I really miss you, too."

"I don't want to hang up," she says. "Maybe now that we understand all this. Maybe now we can be together."

"Dorey, please. Saying that is just another way of hooking in."

"Why couldn't you have said, 'Stay right there, I'm coming to get you?' Now I'm sitting here in this place all alone. I want you. I want you here right now." She is sobbing. "I'm just a big baby. I love you, Alexandra. I love you. Yes. Yes. Why couldn't you have told me absolutely that it would work, that you loved me and would never leave me. Why couldn't you have promised that just now?"

"But Dorey, I can't. We just talked about that."

She is sobbing. "God, quit killing it, will you? Can't you just come and drive me home and we can cry in the car or something and then we can say good-bye? Can't we do it that way?"

"I'm sorry, I can't."

She continues to cry over the phone. "We were going to meet in the next twenty lifetimes and be in love and make love on the floors of various futuristic homes of presidents. Now what happens to those plans, huh? What happens? And I tried to be strong for you. I did try and it didn't work and you said you would give me time. You said it. Now what happens to that plan? What happens to everything between us? Where does it go? Where does it go, Alexandra? Where does it GO?"

"Dorey . . . you said it already. It doesn't disappear. It will go to every person we love."

"Well, you're a traitor to the cause. And I don't go out with traitors."

"Dorey, you're drunk. I'm not having this conversation with you any more."

"Why do you always have to pressure me into being a strong, moral, uplifting, non-fake, non-drunk!"

"I'm sorry," I say. Though I'm not exactly sure why I should be sorry, it seems to be the thing to say.

"I have to go," she says. "I really do have to go. Ann is here. Actually she's been standing at the door for ten minutes now."

"You know you could have told me that before. There's no need to be playing these games. You could have told me she was waiting."

"God, what an egotist you are," she says. "You don't want to go out with me so it's not up to you what I do with Ann, or if I keep her waiting or not."

"Jesus, Dorey, look at this. Look at this shit between us! Will you just look at this shit! It's crazy!" I am exploding with a strange mixture of anger and joy. "God, I love you. I love you and I just want to say that, and I hope to god you have a good life." And then because I don't know what else to say I say, "I love you."

"Yeah," she says softly and that is it.

And I do not hear from her. And that's fine. And I do not wonder so much about her any more, and that's fine too.

It is fall. I am living with Mar-Beth, in the little apartment in the middle of the city. It has a stand-up swimming pool in the back yard, surrounded by a redwood fence with rose climbers. It is a warm fall day and Mar-Beth is down in the swimming pool. I am standing on the back porch, drinking iced tea, leaning over the rail. I can see Mar-Beth's green suit and white legs wavering beneath the water. Her head is on a styrofoam pillow. Another piece of styrofoam holds a drink. She waves when she sees me.

"How's the water?" I shout down.

"Beautiful. Come on! Come in!" she shouts back. She holds up the drink in one hand for me to see. For some reason I don't go in. I just stare. Of course it makes me feel damned alienated. I tell myself it's only temporary.

I do go to Italy. I stand and stare at lots of paintings. I look at lots of mountainsides. I breathe in lots of Mediterranean air.

I leave my mother and Libby one evening to watch the sunset at the beach. I bring Dorey's old letters with me. I read one. "Dear Alex, It seems that life is exploding on us. I heard the phone ringing when you called the other night. Listened to the answering machine, your voice with a tirade of 'where are you's?' And I couldn't answer. God knows, I'm an ass. I couldn't. I'm just failing you all the time, aren't I?

"What do you think of this line— 'I think being nice and mature is just a way of avoiding who I am—which is mean and immature.' Not really. Just schizophrenic. Not really. Just someone who knows too much about life, maybe. I am unhappy without you. I don't know why I didn't pick up that phone. I am so weak and fucking stupid—but just remember—I am brilliant compared to all the others. God, if all this did work out, what would we do for an encore? Are you sick of it yet? Let me know. Until then I am yours in ALL LOVE. I *do* think of us having a horse someday—and a house. Just wanted you to know that. Dorey."

I leave the letters in the sand.

I drink at sidewalk cafes with Libby and my mother. After afternoon siesta we go shopping. We take walks or go to movies at night. We go to the opera or some party they have been invited to. We visit the hotel lounges after midnight and listen to the singers. It is a pleasant numbing. A wash. I think of Dorey while in Italy and what I think is that life and time both work to carry me away from her, and that I should allow it to be so. I should let her go.

And so I don't know how it stopped with Dorey. I don't know what *day* in particular I got tired of it all. I don't know that I really wanted it all to stop. But I do know it stopped. It just stopped. And sometimes

I think, well, if it just stopped, I can just start it again. I can call her and say, "Dorey, I've changed. I'm older now, more mature. We can do it this time, properly. God Dorey, it could be such a full time. Such a fucking full and bloated time. And it could be dizzying!— to 'feel' so much! It could be exhilarating— too much, too much! How often in life is the couple, together, more than what each, alone, can comprehend?"

But I do not make this phone call to Dorey.

I do not.

And when I get home the little swimming pool is filled with leaves, as it is fall, and at some point I finally realize that I am not wondering what Dorey is doing.

And one night I do go for a swim, by myself, with the moonlight edging the walls of the pool, the redwood fence and the geraniums around the pool. There is one cat and one dog sleeping underneath the porch and it is nice, it is peaceful, it is like a dream, it is my own fucking dream, it is mine. I know now that what is mine is there in front of me: the fence, the cat, the dog, the geraniums, the pool, the house, the stars and the sky . . . all mine for this moment . . . and Dorey is not. No, I suppose not. For some reason I feel lucky to have known her, and lucky to be back alive. I feel like god damned Dorothy in Kansas, and I am swimming in the pool and I am new.

*The Crossing Press
publishes a full selection of
feminist titles.
To receive our current catalog,
please call —Toll Free—800/777-1048.*